The Great Squirrel Uprising

A Richard Jackson Book

THE GREAT SQUIRREL UPRISING

DAN ELISH

illustrated by DENYS CAZET

ORCHARD BOOKS NEW YORK

Orchard Books, 387 Park Avenue South
New York, NY 10016

Manufactured in the United States of America
Book design by Mina Greenstein
The text of this book is set in 12 pt. Meridien.
The illustrations are pencil reproduced in halftone.
10 9 8 7 6 5 4 3 2 1

Library of Congress Cataloging-in-Publication Data
Elish, Dan.
The great squirrel uprising / by Dan Elish;
illustrated by Denys Cazet. p. cm.
Summary: With the help of Sally, a sympathetic ten-year-
old human, Scruff the squirrel leads a consortium of
squirrels and birds in a blockade of New York's Central Park
to protest the litter there.
ISBN 0-531-05995-2. ISBN 0-531-08595-3 (lib. bdg.)
[1. Squirrels—Fiction. 2. Birds—Fiction. 3. Central Park
(New York, N.Y.)—Fiction. 4. New York (N.Y.)—
Fiction. 5. Litter (Trash)—Fiction.] I. Cazet, Denys, ill.
II. Title. PZ7.E4257Gr 1992 [Fic]—dc20 91-27145

This book is for
Madeleine,
Andy,
Jamie,
Emily,
Oliver,
Max,
and the squirrels and pigeons
of New York City's Central Park.

Contents

Principal Characters

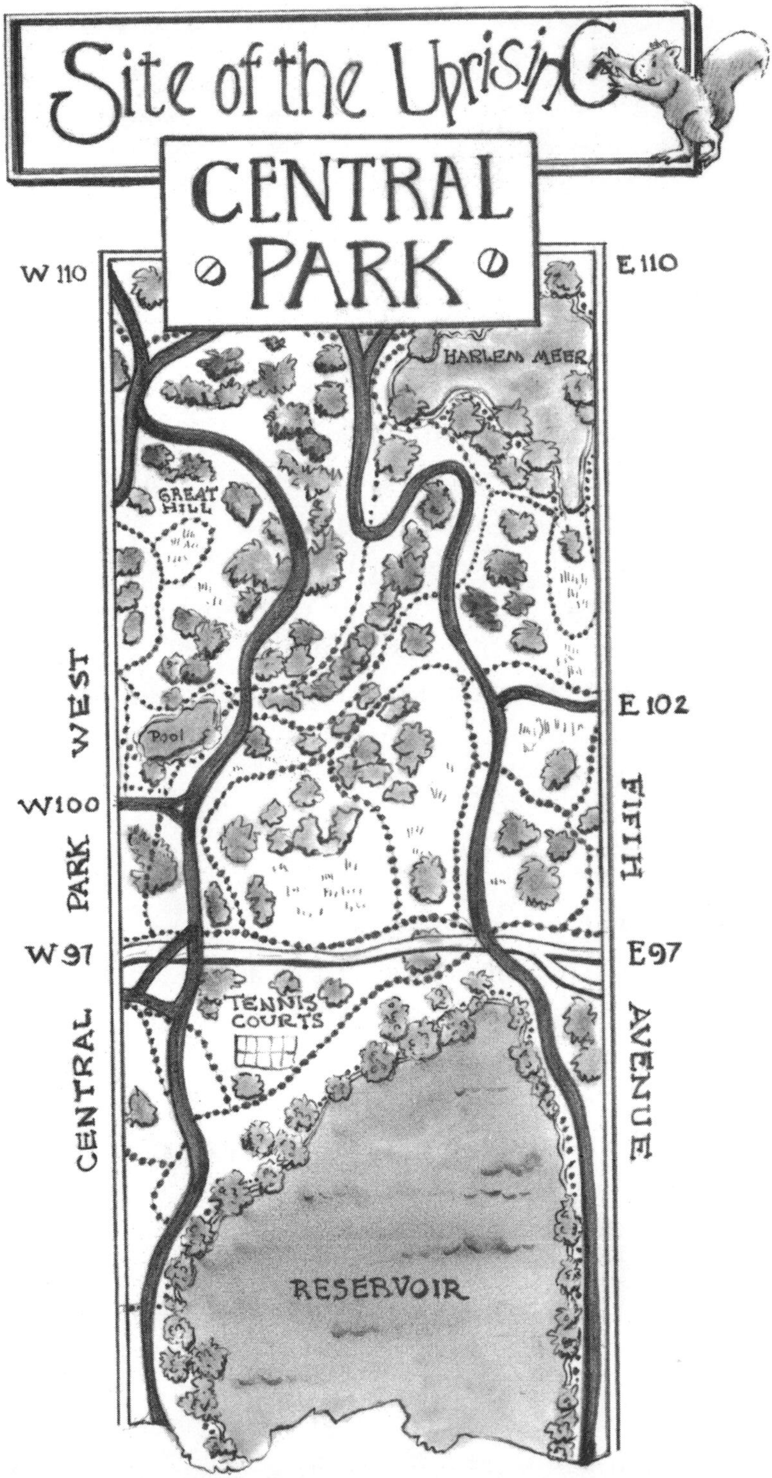

Site of the Uprising

CENTRAL PARK

W 110 E 110

HARLEM MEER

GREAT HILL

Pool

CENTRAL PARK WEST

W 100

W 97

E 102

FIFTH AVENUE

E 97

TENNIS COURTS

RESERVOIR

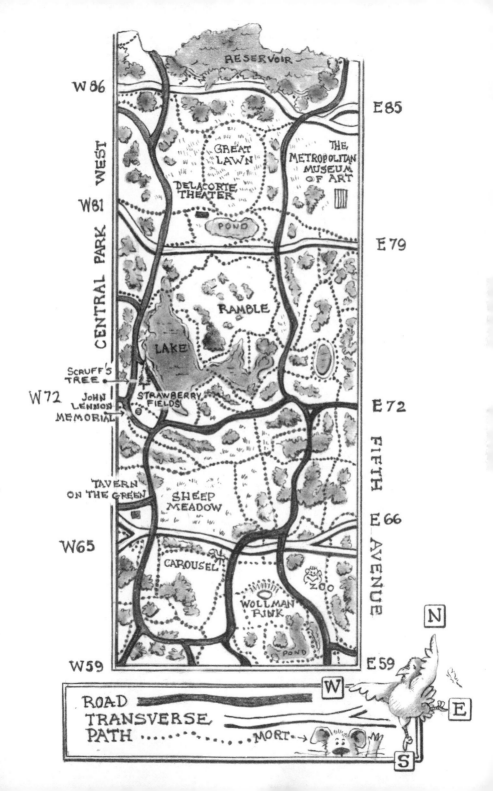

Incident at
West 72nd Street

WITH school finally out, Sally March woke early, polished off some milk and a muffin, rooted her skateboard out of the front closet, and headed for Central Park. She loved its lakes and hilly paths first thing on a Monday morning, after the weekend crowds had gone.

But as soon as she turned right off 73rd Street onto Central Park West, Sally found herself on the edge of a traffic jam. Honks filled the air as two policemen did their best to direct cars away from the park entrance one block to the south.

1

"Aw, come on!" a cabbie complained. "They're only cute rats. Lemme run 'em down."

"Sorry, buddy," a policeman replied. "We got strict orders. It'd make New York City look awfully bad if we let cars squash 'em. For now, the road's closed. Keep movin'!"

Squash what? Sally thought.

An experienced New York traveler, she ran to the corner and cut across the street to the front of a crowd gathered inside the park, beyond the West 72nd Street gateway.

In all her ten years, Sally had never seen anything so amazing. Lined up side by side, linked paw to paw across the road curving into the park, were thirty-two squirrels. She counted them.

"According to today's *Times*, they got organized yesterday evening," a woman behind Sally said with a grin.

Out of the corner of her eye, Sally saw the woman point to a picture of a squirrel with a tuft on his forehead, up on his haunches, glaring into the headlights of a truck. The caption read HEAD SQUIRREL STARES DOWN MOTORIST.

"Pretty brave," a man commented. "But why? Is it some sort of protest?"

Another man chuckled. "Could be," he replied. "But if you ask me, I think they just ate a bad crop of nuts."

Sally turned back to the squirrel she recognized from the photo, who now strutted up and down the blockade line. Flying above him, as if surveying the troops, she saw a white pigeon. To Sally's delight, the bird swooped to rest on the pavement directly in front of her. The squirrel trotted over, smiled broadly, and appeared to start a conversation.

"Look at it, Franklin!" he said to the pigeon. "Have you ever seen anything more beautiful in your life? Hundreds of bewildered humans having no idea what's going on or what to do about it!"

The pigeon eyed the crowd.

"I'm glad you asked me to help out, Scruff. This sure beats hanging around old ladies, waiting for scraps of bread."

Sally was enchanted. Even though she couldn't make out a word, she felt positive the squirrel and the pigeon were talking. She dropped to her knees to listen just as five more squirrels burst out of the bushes and skidded to a halt in front of the leader.

"Reporting for duty, sir," one said.

"Wonderful!" the squirrel chattered. "Now get in line. Shove in if you have to. Pretty soon, about half of you will be moving out to other roads."

As the five raced off, Sally saw a tiny gray mouse poke his head from the undergrowth. He clutched a piece of newspaper in his right paw.

"Other roads?" the mouse exclaimed. "Did I hear you say *other* roads?"

Scruff glanced over his shoulder.

"Mort, Mort, Mort." He sighed. "When are you going to learn that I'm serious? Yes, other roads. *All* of them. And then all the pedestrian pathways. This is an *uprising*, Mort. I plan to take over this park! I've had it!"

"Had it with what?"

"You know with what," the squirrel snapped. "These filthy people! At the end of every hot weekend, it's the exact same thing! Know what I found under my tree last night? A soggy newspaper, three sticky ice cream wrappings, four bent Popsicle sticks, two crushed soda cans, and a shard of glass! It's outrageous! People act as though they own the park when it's *our* home! We're the ones who have to live in their mess!"

"So now you're going to take it over, are you?" The mouse snickered. He shook his head. "Well, in all the history texts I've read, I've never heard of anything crazier."

"Crazy? Well, for once you're going to witness history, not just read about it, Mort, old boy. Once we've won, they'll devote an entire paper—no, whole books—to us."

"Doubtful," Mort observed. "First of all, there aren't enough squirrels who'll join in."

Scruff sat up on his haunches and smiled. "You know," he said, turning to the white pigeon, "I do believe our little friend is jealous."

Mort's whiskers twitched. "Jealous? Me? Of a bunch of squirrels? Don't be ridiculous."

"Yes, jealous," Scruff said, grinning broadly now. "Because squirrels are cute."

"What's that got to do with it?" Mort scoffed. "Mice are cute, too."

"To other mice, maybe," Scruff said. "But not to people. Why, if a group of mice tried to block a road, the humans would pay for the chance to run them down. Don't you think, Franklin?"

The pigeon clucked. "It's quite possible."

Mort clenched his paws. "Okay! Okay! I'll admit that some humans' irrational dislike of my particular species makes it dangerous for me to appear in public. That still doesn't mean that your 'Let's take over the park' idea isn't nuts. You may be able to clog up a few roads, but you'll never keep people out from Fifty-ninth Street to One hundred tenth."

"I don't know about that," Scruff said. "There's Ripper, Scamp, Corker, and many others. If we band together, we'll keep the people out." He looked up and for the first time met Sally's eyes, then raised a paw and pointed to where she sat, watching, just a foot away. "People like that one."

Sally was glowing. Was the squirrel talking to her?

"Hi," she said, shyly.

Scruff snorted. "Did you hear that? 'Hi,' she says. Humans! They ruin our park and then try to be friendly. It never ceases to amaze me!"

Just then, Sally, who had been leaning closer to hear, happened to glance up. Creeping toward the squirrel was a policeman with a large, long-handled net. She jumped to her feet, eyes wide.

"See?" Scruff scoffed, indicating her. "Typical human behavior. Always gaping at something."

The policeman inched nearer. Sally looked around. A few other people watched the officer approaching, but no one moved to help the squirrel. Only a few feet away now, the policeman raised the net over his head, ready to strike. If she didn't warn the animal, Sally knew, no one would. But to do so meant taking sides against the police. Suddenly she didn't care. A squirrel roadblock was too interesting to miss.

She met Scruff's unsuspecting eyes.

"Run!" she cried. "Run for your life!"

2

A Close Call

SCRUFF froze. In a flash, the white pigeon flew forward and batted his wings in the officer's face. Again, Sally shouted, "Run!"

The policeman lunged. Scruff rolled to his side just in time. Ten other policemen, all carrying nets, circled around him.

"Okay," yelled the sergeant in charge. "Take it nice and easy. Let's get this one, and the others'll drift off peacefully."

The crowd pushed close.

"Hold the line!" Scruff cried to the other squirrels. "Whatever happens, don't you dare run!"

"I lay three-to-two odds on the cops!" a man shouted.

Sally clenched her fists. Even though squirrels are much quicker than humans, she knew this squirrel was trapped.

"Leave him alone!" she cried, running forward.

The next thing she knew she was being deposited back on the side of the road by two policemen.

"Stay outta this, okay?" one said.

Scruff considered. If he jumped the line and dashed down the road, he'd head into more police. His best bet was a pedestrian path to his right that led down a hill into a small section of the park called Strawberry Fields. He jerked onto his hind legs and looked both ways. The men with the nets were closing fast.

"Done for already," Mort muttered to himself. "I can't look. . . ."

He ducked into the safety of the undergrowth, then headed back to his hole.

Sally watched from the side of the roadblock, her fingernails digging into her skateboard. She desperately wanted to help. But how? Scruff was poised on the tips of his paws now, ready to sprint. Just then, one squirrel from the middle of the line bolted.

"Get back there!" Scruff commanded.

The squirrel stopped short and stood quivering on its hind legs.

"Back, I say!"

The squirrel scuttled to its former place in the line.

The police were only four feet away . . . three . . . their nets raised over their heads. . . .

"Come on, squirrel!" Sally yelled. "Do something!"

Then she heard a frantic fluttering behind her. The white pigeon again, and followed by at least twenty others! They swooped over her head and into the policemen's faces with a great flapping of wings.

"Run!" Franklin squawked.

Scruff bolted through one policeman's legs and bounded down the pedestrian path. But he wasn't safe yet. More policemen with nets raced after him while others circled down a parallel road to cut him off at the bottom of the hill.

Sally didn't know what to do. But if she could get in *front* of the squirrel, there was something she could try. She suddenly saw a way and, taking a shortcut, crashed through a row of bushes that lined the road. Angling up a narrow cement path, she sped in front of the sprinting squirrel. She could hear the light patter of his paws on the pavement, followed closely by the heavy steps of the police.

"Run, Scruff!" Franklin called, flying above him. "Run!"

"Get that pigeon, too!" Sally heard. "He's one of the ringleaders!"

Sirens wailed. Police cars thundered along the park drives to block Scruff's escape. A net smashed to the ground only inches behind him.

Sally pulled to a stop at the top of a hill and smacked her skateboard down onto a path there. She knew it was crazy, but a skateboard escape was all she could think of. The squirrel was bolting toward her now.

"Get on!" she cried. "Hurry!"

Scruff looked up. That nosy girl again! What in the world was she doing? Blocking his way?

"Jump on!" Franklin shrilled, swooping low to the ground.

Without breaking stride, Scruff leaped in the air and landed on the board. Sally gave him a push, and he went careening wildly down the path.

"Hold on!" Sally cried as the police stormed past.

"That-a-boy, Scruff!" Franklin shouted.

"Gangway!" the squirrel yelled, balancing on his hind legs, riding the board like a surfer.

The hill was steep, and the force of his leap and Sally's push had given him a strong start. The skateboard picked up speed quickly and swerved—

click-clack, click-clack—back and forth down the path.

"Hang ten!" a boy cried.

Scruff neared the bottom.

"Watch it!" the pigeon called.

Before him, Scruff saw a road lined with police cars. The skateboard began shaking uncontrollably, but out of the corner of his eye he spied a tree. He leaned to the right, forcing the board off the path.

Boom!

The squirrel did a backward somersault with a half twist high into the air. Below him, police hastily spread out a large expanse of net. His only chance was to snag a branch. Stretching as far as he could, he reached up with one paw, grabbed . . . and held on. A policeman shook the tree trunk. But Scruff, secure now, scrambled well out of reach.

Sally raced down the hill. She found her skateboard flipped against the tree, its wheels still spinning. Above it, she saw the pigeon settle on the highest branch.

"You all right?" the pigeon asked the squirrel.

Scruff gasped for breath. "Fine, Franklin," he managed. "Fine."

Sally tried hard to catch their coo and chatter from below.

"Young lady?" asked the policeman who had been first with a net. "Have you ever seen this squirrel before?"

"No, sir," she replied.

"Then why did you help it?"

"It seemed fair."

The policeman sighed. "Listen," he said. "That squirrel was obstructing traffic."

"Well, I could see that," Sally said. "But he must have his reasons."

"Humph," the policeman answered. "It's hard enough doing our job in this city without having to psychoanalyze squirrels." He turned back to the others. Then, over his shoulder, he added, "No more meddling, kid."

Sally was worried that somehow the police might go after the squirrel again, maybe call in the fire department with a hook-and-ladder truck. But as she collected her skateboard, she saw the policemen roll up the netting and stuff it into the trunk of one of the patrol cars. They seemed to be calling it quits.

Up in the tree, Scruff grinned. "New York's finest," he said, "aren't New York's fastest. Right, Franklin, old friend?"

"Right," the pigeon agreed. "But what about that girl? Pretty smart for a human, huh? She saved your life."

Scruff glared down at Sally, who was squinting to find him and Franklin among the leaves.

"I know! I know!" he said. "Don't remind me!"

3

All the News
That's Fit To Rip

"So, how are the troops?" Scruff asked, changing the subject.

"I'll check 'em out," said Franklin, flying into the air. In just minutes, he was back. "Looking good. Police are keeping their distance. And a friend tells me reinforcements are heading south from around One hundred eighth Street. So the news is spreading."

"Excellent! I doubt the police will try anything, but it might be wise if I wait in this tree a while before showing my all too distinctive face."

14

"What about the girl?" Franklin asked, nodding in her direction. Sally had taken a seat on a bench by the tree.

"The what?"

The pigeon drew a deep breath, summoning all his courage. "You know, Scruff, I was thinking . . . you really ought to thank her."

Scruff scrunched up his brow in disgust. "*Thank her?* Franklin, it's not in my nature to thank humans for anything. You know that."

"I know," Franklin said. "But, if your plan is to work—if we're really going to block off the entire park—you'll need *some* human help. For instance, who'll communicate with the other humans in the city? Who'll advise you as to human ways of doing things?" The pigeon glanced down at Sally. "She obviously likes us."

Scruff stared into space, turning over the notion in his mind. He thought he knew well the human ways of doing things.

"But—" he began.

"You know I've got a point," Franklin cut in.

Scruff shook his head. "All right," he said finally. "This girl may well be able to help. Fly off and find Mort. I'll lure her over there." He gestured toward a playing field, where dew still sparkled on the grass.

"Good," Franklin said. "I'll join you in a minute."

The pigeon took wing. "And Scruff," he called back. "Be nice to her!"

Sally looked up at the sound of Franklin's soft coo.

"Okay! Okay!" the squirrel replied, inching down the tree. "But don't you dare tell anyone about this, Franklin! I have a reputation to maintain!"

Scruff checked both ways for police, then dashed to the ground. Seconds later, he stood in front of Sally.

"Hi," she said, with a grin. "That was a close call before."

She wasn't sure, but it seemed that the squirrel was nodding.

"You're creating quite a commotion, aren't you?"

Scruff gestured with his paws and then began to walk, very slowly, toward the field. When Sally realized that he was leading her, she felt giddy. She picked up her skateboard, sidestepped two bikers, and followed. But after Scruff had taken a few steps, she saw him shudder at the sight of an empty grape juice container on the grass. With two quick leaps, he was grabbing at it furiously. But try as he might, he couldn't get a good enough grip to carry it up the side of a nearby trash can.

"Let me," Sally said, reaching out to him.

Up on his haunches, Scruff watched Sally toss the container into the can.

16

Oh, great! he thought, continuing across the street. One of those "pretend I care" humans!

Sally caught up with him just as Franklin fluttered in for a landing. Then she saw the mouse dash between some bushes, hide behind a tree at the edge of the field, look both ways, and finally scoot toward them.

"This had better be important, Scruff," the mouse said. "I was deep into a book I found called *Presidential Trivia*. And William Taft, our country's fattest president, just got stuck in his bathtub."

"It's good to see you, too, Mort," Scruff replied. "Important? Well, I guess so. I need your assistance in introducing me to this girl."

The mouse raised his eyebrows, interested against his will.

"Do my ears deceive me?" he asked. "The squirrel who despises humans actually wants to meet one?"

"That's right," Scruff said. "And if you tell anyone, I'll wrap your stringy tail around your neck!"

Mort peered at Sally, who was watching them patiently, fascinated.

"You know, I didn't stay up nights teaching myself to read to make your life easier," he remarked to the squirrel.

"She saved Scruff's life," Franklin said.

"Enough of that already!" Scruff glared at the pigeon.

Sally caught the glint in his eyes.

"Well, I don't care whose life she saved," Mort said, turning away. "All I want is to be left to read in peace."

"My point exactly!" Scruff said. "When this park is ours, you'll have peace and quiet enough to read all day long! Think of the books you could finish, Mort! Why, you might even find time to write one."

"And I'd have the perfect story," the mouse replied. "All about a crazy squirrel—"

Scruff smirked. "—who ate a stubborn mouse. Now get moving!"

Mort sighed and disappeared into the bushes, just as a Frisbee landed near Scruff.

"These flying disks!" he complained to Franklin. "Another human annoyance!"

Sally tossed the Frisbee to a waiting teenage girl as Mort reappeared, dragging three crumpled pieces of newspaper.

"Okay," he said. "Let's hurry up. It's getting hot out here."

Franklin swooped down and landed on Sally's shoulder, surprising her. He gestured to the ground where the mouse sat with the pieces of paper. Her heart pounding, she nodded and knelt down.

"Whose name shall we do first?" Mort said.

"How about yours?" Scruff replied.

Sally watched the mouse creep onto the newspaper and pace back and forth, working his way slowly down the page.

"Find anything?" Scruff asked.

Mort looked up.

"Don't rush me," he said. "Not many people have the good fortune to be called Mort, you know. Let's see. No, not that. Maybe . . . no, no. That wouldn't do. Wait. Here we go! Yes!"

Mort carefully spread before him a headline that read OIL ON THE BEACHES—RESIDENTS MORTIFIED.

Then he pointed his tiny front paws at the final word. Sally had no idea what the animals were trying to show her. The pigeon and squirrel kept pointing at the mouse and the mouse kept pointing at MORTIFIED. She wrinkled her brow. Animals can't read, she thought. What are they doing?

"See?" Mort said, after a minute. "What did you expect? It doesn't work."

"Tear your name out," Scruff said.

"What?"

"Tear it out!"

"But it's my pap—"

"Tear it out!"

"Ah, why not?" the mouse said. "It's yester-day's."

Soon, Mort had ripped the word MORTIFIED down to MORTI. Then he stood on his hind legs, facing Sally, and held it up against his chest.

"Morty?" Sally said. "Your name is Morty!"

Sally blinked and then looked at the animals wide-eyed. This was incredible! These animals, or at least one of them, could read!

"She's got it!" Scruff cried.

"Good job!" Franklin cooed.

"Only the name is Mort. Not Morty!"

"Morty's cuter," Scruff said. "Now come on. Let's teach her my name next."

This one took more effort. Finally, after much fussing, Mort found two articles, one with the phrase "The wood was rough," and another with the headline SCRANTON BEATS POUGHKEEPSIE. Carefully, he ripped off the word "rough" and the letters Sc and placed them side by side.

"Scruff!" Sally said. "Hi, Scruff."

The name Franklin was easy. In the TV section, Mort found a listing for an after-school special about Benjamin Franklin. He pointed at the name, and they were all set.

"Franklin, Morty, and Scruff," Sally said. "And my name's Sally."

"All right, then," Scruff said. "We're done. If we need her, we'll call her. And, *Morty*, old budderoo, keep those newspapers handy. We'll be needing you now and again."

"Lucky, *lucky* me," the mouse complained.

"Oh, lighten up," Scruff said, heading back to the roadblock. "Who knows? If you get friendly enough, maybe she'll lend you some good books."

20

An Open Window

SALLY spent the afternoon skateboarding in a happy daze. After all, she was, as far as she knew, the first person outside of a story to actually communicate with a mouse!

When she returned to the apartment, her mother was listening to the day's last piano student.

"Hey, guess what?" Sally said, appearing in the living room.

"What?" her mother asked.

"Well, it's really no big deal," Sally began. "I mean, I don't want to interrupt your lesson with it. But since you asked . . . did you hear about those squirrels on West Seventy-second? Well, I was there this morning when some policemen tried to get the head squirrel with these nets. So I yelled, 'Watch it,' and the pigeon—he's a white one—flew into one cop's face and the squirrel jumped away just in time! Then all the police chased the squirrel, but I shoved my skateboard in front of him, and he got away."

Mrs. March shivered. "You *helped* the squirrel?"

"That's right," Sally said. "And then—later on, that is—the squirrel, pigeon, and mouse (oh, there's this mouse, too) introduced themselves by ripping pieces of the newspaper!"

Sally, breathless, glowed with excitement.

"Anthony," Mrs. March said vaguely to her student. "That's all for today."

Anthony shoved his music into his book bag and hustled out the door, nearly knocking over Mr. March, who was on his way in.

"Hi, Dad!" Sally cried, racing into his arms. "Did you hear about the squirrels?"

"Sure, I did! But did you hear they've moved?"

Mrs. March stood up. "They what?"

"Moved," Mr. March said. "It's all here in the afternoon paper."

"But I just came from the park," Sally said. "They were still at West Seventy-second Street."

"That's correct," her father replied. "But now there's also a group uptown."

Mr. March held out the paper. In the middle of the front page was a picture of a roadblock and a headline reading SQUIRRELS SCURRY TO 77TH STREET!

Mrs. March's upper lip twitched. "They're taking over the city. . . ."

"And it seems they've had the help of a little girl."

"You mean . . . Sally?" her mother exclaimed. "How do you know about it?"

"Simple. It's all on page three."

Her hands shaking, Mrs. March opened the paper. There, in black and white, was her daughter pushing a squirrel on a skateboard down a hill. The caption beneath the picture read MYSTERY SKATEBOARD GIRL SAVES SQUIRREL. Sally's mother skimmed the article quickly, murmuring aloud as she read: " 'The head squirrel, surrounded by nets . . . put down her skateboard . . . police looking for another opportunity to catch said squirrel . . . city is amused . . . mayor plans no immediate action. . . .' "

When she was through, Mrs. March took a deep breath and slumped onto the sofa.

"Honey," she said to Sally. "I know you love animals, but this is a serious matter. Squirrels can carry diseases. Whatever happened to playing with humans? Isn't Sheila home? Can't you spend your free time with her?"

"She's left for camp."

"Oh. Then how about Jill?"

"She's gone to Rhode Island with her parents."

"Well, then, I don't know, how about . . . Heavens! What's that? A pigeon? In my clean living room?"

"Franklin!" Sally cried.

Indeed, it was. The pigeon had followed Sally home and then flown up ten stories to her apartment. Sally ran toward the window ledge. Franklin swooped onto her wrist. Mrs. March leaped up, hand over mouth, while Mr. March retrieved the newspaper, ready to wave it at the bird in case he came too close.

"Please, Sally," her father said. "You know we respect your friendship with all animals, but we don't approve of them dropping in for dinner. Now, shoo him out."

Unseen by her parents, Franklin opened his beak and deposited a tiny piece of paper in Sally's hand. His mission complete, he fluttered to the window and . . . then back to the park.

"See? No big deal. He's gone."

Mrs. March collapsed onto the piano bench. "Sally," she said. "If the friends you like are already away for the summer, fine. But from now on, if you care to socialize with animals, you must do so outside."

"Right, Mom," Sally said. "I'll go wash up for dinner now."

Once alone, she opened her fist. For a second, she simply stared at a small crumpled piece of newspaper. Her heart racing, she spread it out on the bathroom counter.

CITYWIDE LIFE INSURANCE
WISHES TO THANK ITS CUSTOMERS.

What was this? Why had the pigeon gone to the trouble of giving her a life insurance ad? Was it a mistake? Quickly, Sally turned the paper over. The other side appeared to be an ad for running shoes. She flipped the paper back and read the words aloud once more. Suddenly their meaning became clear: Franklin was thanking her for saving Scruff's life!

Sally leaned out the small bathroom window. Looking up 73rd Street, she could see the green outlines of Central Park.

One day, two roads blocked . . .

Sally didn't know exactly what the animals were up to. But whatever it was, she wanted to be a part of it.

⎚5

Day Two

By 6:00 A.M. on Tuesday, the sun was fingering the treetops overhead. During the night, Scruff had organized a third roadblock and given command to Ripper, his cousin and leader of a band of squirrels from the east side of the park.

"Now you know what to do," Scruff told him. "When the first car comes, all fifty of you grasp paws and don't move!"

"Fear not!" Ripper declared. "Motorized vehicles have never fazed us!"

Just then, a yellow cab signaled to turn right off Fifth Avenue.

"Well, here's your chance to prove it," Scruff called, bounding to the edge of the road to watch.

"Okay, troops!" Ripper called from the center of the line as the cab squealed toward them. "Stand tall and hold paws! That's it! Closer together down there! Excellent! Now, for the good name of Central Park—nobody move!"

Not a squirrel flinched. The cabdriver screeched to a halt inches from the line.

"Child's play!" Ripper said with a grin.

"Good stuff!" Scruff yelled, and dashed back across the park for more recruits.

THE mayor of New York arrived at City Hall that morning to find a group of reporters waiting.

"Mr. Mayor," one began. "The squirrels just took *East* Seventy-second Street! What do you think they want?"

"Since no one in the city can speak to them, it's impossible to say," the mayor replied with a smile and a nod of his bald head as he strode into his office and took a seat behind his desk. "If I could get hold of a Squirrel-English dictionary, I'd ask them myself."

The reporters chuckled softly as the mayor opened his briefcase, took out a bag of doughnuts, and after poking at several, picked up a creme filled.

"You don't seem overly concerned, sir. Will you resort to force to clear the animals away?"

"Of course not," the mayor asserted, sniffing his doughnut. "It's time the world saw New Yorkers as they really are—good-hearted souls who would never lift a finger to hurt a fellow citizen."

"Will this squirrel problem affect your reelection campaign?"

"Indeed. I hope to get the vote of every animal in the city. Now if that's all, I'd like to concentrate on my breakfast."

IT didn't take long for word of the squirrels' progress to spread.

"I think they're cute," a businesswoman told a reporter that day over lunch. "Last night I dreamed the head squirrel was elected mayor and made us pay taxes in acorns!"

"Hey, New York has far too many cars in it as it is," a construction worker declared. "I say put a row of squirrels in front of the Lincoln Tunnel and the George Washington Bridge and let 'em close off the whole town."

"This is big," a bookstore owner announced that afternoon. "Any book having anything to do with squirrels has already sold out! I'll tell you—these animals are serious business!"

28

In fact, by noon that day, squirrels had already been painted on coffee mugs, T-shirts, pillowcases, socks, lampshades, ski boots, pencil sharpeners, tweezers—anything—and rushed into stores.

And that was only the beginning.

A woman made a fortune taking pictures of passersby posing with a huge cardboard replica of Scruff.

The Museum of Natural History threw together an exhibit on squirrel evolution.

A punk rock group, previously called The Orange Goats, dyed their hair gray and changed their name to The Squirrel Heads. Their new single, "Be a Squirrel—Everybody's Doing It," was climbing the charts by midafternoon.

"WE'RE making real progress," Scruff observed proudly toward dusk. "We've got over six hundred more recruits already!"

He cast his eyes over Sheep Meadow, an expanse of grass near West 65th Street. In the distance, a group of girls and boys played softball.

"We have done well," Franklin agreed, as a man strode by, leading a well-groomed poodle on a leash. "And don't forget—we can use pigeons, too."

Scruff's eyes went wide. "Pigeons?"

"That's right."

"You must be joking," Scruff said.

"It's no joke. You're going to need all the help you can get, aren't you?"

"Well, sure," Scruff admitted. "But no offense, Franklin . . . I mean, let's face it: pigeons are cowards. Always fluttering off. Scattering in panic. You're an exception, of course, but can you imagine a row of them holding strong before oncoming cars and trucks?"

"I can," Franklin said. "Pigeons are just as brave as squirrels."

"Just as brave as squirrels?" Scruff shook his head. "Now I *know* you're joking. Franklin, in case you haven't noticed, Mother Nature has blessed the squirrel with extraordinary gifts: speed, agility, and power—not to mention courage."

Franklin ruffled his feathers. "Good grief! You're an even bigger swellhead than I thought."

"Swellhead? Me?"

"Yes, you. And your exclusive squirrels-only attitude is going to undermine the cause if you're not careful."

"What's that supposed to mean?"

"Just this. If you really feel it would be too degrading for a breed of creature as glorious as your own to join forces with a flock of pigeons, that's fine. But don't come crying to me when you run short of recruits. Don't forget, Scruff, you've set yourself an enormous goal: to take over the park, the *whole* thing. That's eight hundred forty-three acres! You're going to have to block it off with something, and I don't mean cockroaches."

Scruff scowled. "Very funny. I'll do what I—"

"I've done some figuring," Franklin cut in. "There are at least one hundred roads and paths into the park. It takes thirty or more squirrels to block each one. That means you'll need roughly three thousand squirrels! There's no way you can round up that many."

Scruff fiddled with his paws. "Well . . . I never claimed to be good at math. . . . Three thousand, you say? Hmmm . . . maybe we could get . . ."

"Scruff." Franklin fluttered in front of his friend. His voice softened. "You need every pigeon you can get and you know it."

Scruff met Franklin's eyes, shook himself, and paced. "Pigeons? Block a road with . . . with *pigeons* . . . a bunch of birds?"

"Well?" Franklin asked finally.

Scruff wheeled around. "But do you really think they'll be up to it?"

Franklin shot his friend a look.

Scruff shrugged. "Oh, all right. Round up whoever you can. But those pigeons better not let me down! If there's anything I hate it's—"

Just then, Sally, who had spent most of the day chasing after the squirrel and bird, ran up from behind with her skateboard.

"Hey, Scruff! Franklin!"

Scruff winced. *"Her* again!" he exclaimed.

"Hi," Sally said. Franklin flew to her shoulder. "Hello, Franklin. Thanks for the visit last night."

Scruff opened and shut his eyes. "You visited her?"

The pigeon nodded.

Scruff sighed, clenching his paws. "No wonder she's been following us around. Why in the world did you do that?"

"I felt like it," the pigeon said. "So?"

"Creates the wrong impression! When you hang around with a human it sets a bad example for—"

Just then, Scruff caught sight of the leader of the Sheep Meadow squirrels. "Corker! *There* you are!" he cried. "How goes it?"

"No complaints," Corker replied, bounding up a bit out of breath. "Word has it you've been busy."

"Oh, yes," Scruff said, smiling. "We've been having a ball. And how about you joining our fun?"

By this time, a dozen other squirrels had gathered behind Corker. Delighted to be watching, Sally sat down a short distance away.

"Tell me," Corker said. "Is that the girl who helped you escape yesterday?"

Scruff waved his paw. "She's unimportant. Listen, we've already blocked three roads and—"

"What was that thing she put under you?" Corker asked, gazing intently now at Sally.

"Thing?" Scruff asked, rising on his hind legs. "What thing?"

Corker grinned. "The thing with wheels."

"It's a skateboard," Franklin volunteered.

Sally leaned forward on her knees, thrilled that the small dark eyes of a dozen squirrels were focused on her.

"An interesting device," another squirrel commented, inching toward Sally.

"Yes, yes," Scruff said. "I suppose so, but about joining—"

"You see," Corker said, "we'd like a chance— that is, some of the younger ones here would like a chance to ride."

Scruff cocked his head. "A chance to ride . . . the skateboard?"

Corker's black eyes sparkled. "That's right."

A younger squirrel took an eager step forward. "Oh, can we, Father?"

"But I came here to talk about—" Scruff began.

"We know what you came to talk about," Corker said. "And we aren't entirely interested. Oh, it's not that we don't believe in your cause— humans certainly are messy—it's just that it's too darned hot to stand on a road all day."

"Hot!" Scruff exclaimed, beginning to pace.

"Of course it's hot. But what's a little discomfort? Humans have made our home unlivable. It's time we make a stand!"

"Wait a second," Franklin said, gliding to the ground next to him. "Let's not fight. How about we get Sally to give Corker's kids a skateboard ride in exchange for his joining the uprising?"

"That's insane!" Scruff fumed.

"Hey," Franklin said. "We were just talking about the need for three thousand squirrels, Scruff. Shouldn't we do whatever we can to get them?"

"Yeah . . . but using humans?"

"Please, Mr. Scruff, sir," the youngest squirrel piped up. "We've simply got to ride the wheeled board."

Scruff and Corker locked eyes.

"Well," Scruff said, "I guess I've got no choice but to accept more human help. If it's okay with you, it's okay with me. Rides for recruits."

"It's a deal," said Corker.

The two squirrels shook paws.

"Yippee!" the younger squirrels cried, and in a mad dash, surrounded Sally.

"Hey!" she yelped, standing up with a start.

But then she felt the light touch of Franklin again on her shoulder.

"Back off a little," the pigeon told the squirrels. "You'll scare her."

He cooed softly into Sally's ear and flew a few feet away, as if asking her to join him. One squirrel stepped aside, and then the others followed as she started toward the edge of the meadow. She guessed now at what was expected and placed her skateboard on the cement path.

The first squirrel hopped aboard. Sally smiled and pushed lightly with her foot. The skateboard began slowly, but quickly picked up speed.

"Gangway!" Sally yelled, running behind.

Near the bottom, the squirrel jumped off. Sally retrieved the board and brought it back up for the next.

"Oh, thank you, Father," the first young squirrel shrieked, rushing over to Corker. "I loved it! It went *clickity-clack* all the way down! And it was so fast!"

Corker patted his son's head and smiled at Scruff.

"So, what road do you want us to block first?"

Just then, Sally's voice rang through the air.

"All right!" she cried, racing alongside the second young squirrel. "Good job!"

Scruff scowled in Sally's direction. That girl and her silly skateboard had helped him again.

"I'll get back to you," he told Corker.

"Hey, squirrel!"

Scruff looked up. It was the poodle he had seen

earlier. His master had joined a small crowd of people watching the skateboarding.

"*Human* help to take over the park?" The dog smirked. "Pretty pathetic, isn't it?"

Scruff was furious. The last thing he needed now was abuse from a poodle.

"Oh, go home and eat a milk bone, you plucked beast! I'll run my uprising however I like!"

"Come, Griswald," the dog's master said, and pulled the poodle along.

"Leashed animals!" Scruff groaned to Corker. "They're almost as bad as humans!"

With a pointed look toward Sally, he bounded off across the meadow.

"Scruff!" she called.

But he did not pause. Corker watched him go.

That squirrel, he thought, what a piece of work! and turned toward the skateboarders. Sally was getting ready to give a third ride.

"All right, everyone!" he announced. "My turn!"

"*Father!*"

Suddenly, the eyes of all the young squirrels were focused on him. Corker grinned in embarrassment. "Well . . . I guess I'll get to the end of the line. . . ."

Overnight News

"RISE and shine," Franklin called excitedly the next morning.

Mort's sleepy face poked out of his hole. "Isn't it nighttime?"

"Nope," Franklin replied. "The sun's at the top of the Empire State Building."

"Well, down here it's still dark. Come back in an hour."

"But listen. Just rip me a message for Sally and you can go back to bed. I want to tell her we've blocked every road into the park!"

The mouse's eyes went wide. "Every road? But how?"

Franklin grinned. "Pigeon power."

"Pigeon power?"

"You heard me. As soon as Sally was done giving skateboard rides, I flew to all the rooftops and apartment ledges I could find. And word spread more quickly than I dreamed. By sunset, hundreds of pigeons were on their way to Sheep Meadow to await Scruff's orders. I tell you, Mort, it was a pretty sight—all those birds fluttering up from the horizon, soaring through the orange sky."

"*Thrilling*, I'm sure," Mort remarked with a yawn. "I'd love to hear the rest, but let's save it for a more civilized hour."

The mouse ducked back into his hole. He soon reappeared carrying a small piece of paper.

"Here," he said. "And from now on, please bear in mind that I am *not* an early riser."

As the mouse's tail disappeared again down his hole, Franklin pecked up the message and glided out of the park, across Central Park West. The streetlights were still on, and except for the rattle of a garbage truck and the dim hum of a bus, the city was quiet.

The pigeon came to rest at a sill on 73rd Street. He peered in at the open window.

The room was pale. Sally lay on her back, sound

asleep. Franklin flew to the side of her bed, but just as he was reaching to nudge her with his wing, he spotted something on the dresser—a radio. Interested, he hopped over.

He dropped the paper, flicked a switch, and adjusting the volume to low, pressed his head close to the speaker. He moved the station dial until he recognized a Mozart symphony, then began swaying back and forth, soaking up the sounds. Franklin loved classical music. Every summer, he had listened to the New York Philharmonic play free concerts in the park's Great Lawn. And once he'd flown all the way to Brooklyn's Prospect Park to hear a performance of Beethoven's Sixth.

Sally stirred, shifted her head on her pillow, and opened her eyes.

"Franklin?" she exclaimed.

The bird snapped out of his trance, retrieved Mort's message, and settled on Sally's stomach.

"You like music?"

Franklin cooed, and Sally reached for whatever it was that he carried in his beak. She saw that, as before, it was a scrap of newspaper.

" 'Head squirrel and pigeon blocked . . .' " she read, then looked up. "That's all?"

Franklin fluttered to the pillow and looked at the note. Though he couldn't read, the pigeon suspected that Mort, in his haste to get back to bed, had accidentally misripped the paper. For what was printed didn't look long enough to convey the whole message.

At that moment, Sally's door swung open. She saw her father in his pajamas, silhouetted against the light from the hall.

"Well, well, well," he said. "What have we here? Another meeting?"

Sally looked pleadingly at him. Franklin blinked.

"You won't tell Mom?"

Mr. March sat on the edge of Sally's bed.

"This pigeon seems to like you. And what is this? A bit of paper?"

"Yes, Dad," Sally replied. "You see, Franklin here brought me this note from the mouse I told you about. From Morty. The trouble is, I can't figure it out."

"Well," her father said, looking it over. "It's hard to interpret the messages of a mouse and pigeon."

"I hope it's not that Scruff is angry at me."

"Angry? Why?"

"Remember, I told you I gave skateboard rides to those squirrels? Well, Scruff sure took off in a hurry. And before he went, he gave me a nasty look."

Mr. March sighed. "You know, Sally, you'll

find that in life there are times when you try to do something nice and it doesn't go the way you mean it to. Once I told a friend at the office that he looked thin, and he said, 'So I was fat before?' Another time, I took my boss's son to a ball game, and he got hit in the elbow by a foul ball. Let's hope that Scruff'll see you were only trying to help."

He patted Sally's head. "One thing," he said as he stood up and walked toward the door. "You'd better not bring that pigeon in for breakfast. I have a feeling your mother might not understand."

"YOUR father tells me you were listening to Mozart this morning," Mrs. March said at the kitchen table. "I never knew you liked classical music."

"Oh, yes," Sally replied. "The older I get, the more I appreciate the great composers."

Her mother smiled. "Why, that's *fine.*"

"Will you look at this?" Mr. March said, closing the front door. "Here, on the front page."

"What's it say?" his wife asked.

"PARKBLOCK! the headline says. They've taken over all the roads!"

Sally's eyes widened. So that's what Franklin had meant to tell her.

"I've got to see this!" she cried.

"No, you don't," her mother said. "Not until after breakfast."

"Okay. But read it, Dad, please," Sally said.

As she poured milk on her cereal, her father took a seat at the table and began on page one.

" 'The squirrels expanded dramatically upon their two-day uprising last night, blocking every entrance to the road that circles the interior of Central Park.

" 'Impressively organized, the squirrels, now joined by hundreds of pigeons, systematically closed off road after road, working up the West Side to One hundred tenth Street, around Central Park North, down Fifth Avenue to Fifty-ninth Street, along Central Park South, and back up Central Park West to their starting point at Seventy-second Street. Pedestrian paths in and out of the park have not been affected.

" ' "It's certainly a surprise," the deputy mayor admitted this morning on his way to a doughnut breakfast meeting at Gracie Mansion. "But one thing's for sure. The mayor won't use force against the animals. He's firm about that."

" 'Most surprising to experts is the participation of the pigeons. Until last night, it was assumed that, except for the white bird, the squirrels were acting on their own.

" ' "Who'd have guessed the birds would help," David McGarry, a park ranger, said. "Pigeons generally look out only for themselves. I just didn't think they would sign on for a group project like this."

" 'The pigeons have proved themselves more than equal to the undertaking. On East Ninetieth Street, a road blocked only by birds, not a feather fluttered in the face of oncoming traffic. As elsewhere around the park, cabs, cars, trucks, even police vehicles ground to a halt.

" ' "We've got orders to keep the cars away from the animals," said one fed-up-sounding policeman at One hundred tenth and Central Park West. "But I tell you, if this uprising lasts, the weekend's not gonna be easy." ' "

Mr. March put down the paper. Sally put down her spoon.

"Now may I?" she asked.

Her father nodded.

Her mother sighed. "All right," she said. "Have fun. Say hello to the squirrels for us."

"And don't forget your skateboard," Mr. March called after her. "You never know when it might come in handy!"

7

Trouble
in the
Ranks

THE moment Sally stepped from her building onto 73rd Street, she was greeted by a din of shouts and honks. Traffic was bumper-to-bumper.

"Are the squirrels causing this?" she asked Mike, her doorman.

"Who else?" he replied. "With the roads to the park closed, more cars have to use the side streets."

West 72nd Street was clogged with police, reporters, and onlookers. Vendors hawked HEAD SQUIRREL FOR MAYOR T-shirts. A woman wearing a squirrel mask sold bags of roasted peanuts. And members of The Animal Rights League passed out pamphlets entitled SQUIRRELS AND YOU—PERFECT TOGETHER.

Sally moved quickly to the front of the crowd. The squirrels she saw looked a little weary. She wasn't surprised, considering that today was Wednesday and most of them had been standing in the same place for two days without a break. Three squirrels traveled the line, dropping the morning's ration of one acorn in front of each animal.

Just then, Franklin swooped down to Sally's shoulder.

"Hi," she said to the bird. "Now I know what that note was meant to tell me! You blocked all the roads!" She looked back at the blockade, her eyes wide with wonder, almost as though she were seeing it for the first time. "It's unbelievable!"

Franklin brushed her face with his wing just as she saw Scruff poke his head out of the undergrowth, glance both ways for police, and bound into the open. Franklin swooped to the squirrel's side.

Sally stepped closer. Though she couldn't make out his meaning, she could tell Scruff had something urgent to say.

"Friends," he began, striding up and down the

line of squirrels. "You are to be congratulated! We are well on our way to our goal: ridding this park of humans, of the unruly throngs just behind me here."

Scruff gestured and caught sight of Sally. His tail twitched.

"And when we've finished the job," he continued, now rising to his haunches and gesturing broadly, "this park will be a garden again in the middle of the city. A place where animals can live together in peace, without cars, noise, or litter. Picture it!" His black eyes sparkled. "A park where squirrels and all park creatures can sit together in peace at the Great Lawn at Eighty-first Street. A park where a squirrel couple can have friends over to their tree without being interrupted by a rock concert! A park where a squirrel can cross a road and not risk getting flattened!"

He paused and then, in a voice quivering with emotion, orated:

"We squirrels, we happy few—we band of brothers. For he today who blocks this road with me shall *be* my brother forever and ever!"

Trembling, Scruff gazed steadfastly along the line. Some squirrels rubbed paws to their eyes. He turned to Franklin. "Do you want to follow along?"

"Where?" the bird asked.

"To keep me company while I give more speeches. You can deliver one to the pigeons, if you like. Generals must be seen by their troops! Come on!"

As the squirrel turned downtown, Franklin signaled to Sally. She got on her skateboard and hurried behind.

AND so a long morning of speechmaking began.

Franklin went first, addressing a row of pigeons blockading a road on Central Park South. "I know that your claws ache," he began, puffing out his chest and flapping his wings, "that your stomachs growl, that you miss your apartment ledges, that your feathers are frayed. But please, remember: alone, a pigeon may be weak, but united, we are stronger than the mightiest truck!"

And later, at East 59th, across the street from the Plaza Hotel, Scruff stood high on his back legs and intoned, "Brave squirrels! Courageous birds! Now is the summer of our discontent! Give me the park! Or give me death!"

But eloquence alone couldn't make the day cooler or the concrete more cushioned. As the temperature rose, the roadblocking troops grew fidgety and disheartened. Sally saw many squirrels and pigeons gaze longingly toward the comfort of the park's trees, grass, and shade only a few hops away.

Scruff seemed unaware of any possible effect the heat might be having. Midmorning found him in a fine mood.

"What a day to be a leader!" he exclaimed to Franklin as the two made their way toward East 66th Street. Sally stayed close on her skateboard. "The sun is bright, the troops strong! Why, I shouldn't be surprised if—"

He paused, and his body went rigid. Up ahead, he saw two little squirrels from the end of the line dash from the road and take a running leap onto a drinking fountain.

"Hey!" Scruff cried, charging forward. "You know the rules! One at a time for drinks! And use the lake!"

But the squirrels were gnawing at the faucet. Sally skateboarded over and pressed the button for them.

"Thirsty, huh?"

They drank greedily and ducked their faces under the spray. But then Sally heard scrambling paws on the pavement behind her. She turned just in time to see a bushy gray tail disappear into the undergrowth. A deserter.

"What in the world is going on here?" Scruff cried, tearing after the runaway. "Get back in line! Back, I say!"

But Scruff lost him at the edge of the trees. He barreled back to the line just as the two squirrels from the drinking fountain scurried back to their positions.

"I hope no one else has ideas about following that squirrel's cowardly example!" Scruff exclaimed, gesturing toward the trees behind him. "So it's a tad warm. So what? You all have been called to participate in the worthiest of causes! Saving our park!"

As Scruff spoke, Sally saw that, despite the heat, every squirrel now stood at attention. But no new squirrel had come to replace the one who had bolted. One gap in the line might become two . . . three . . . four. . . . How long would it take before a car could squeeze through?

"Looks like you guys need some backups," she said to Franklin, who was perched on a nearby bench.

The bird cooed and cocked his head as Scruff stormed into the tail end of his speech.

"The humans aren't going to roll over and play dead!" he asserted, stamping on the cement for emphasis. "But, brave friends, I know you are up to the challenge! Never forget that you are a squirrel, the most courageous creature on earth!"

"Hey," Franklin called as Scruff, finished now, marched their way. "Sally just made a good point."

"The last thing I need at the moment," he snapped, "is advice from a girl."

But as the morning grew hotter, Scruff discovered a group of pigeons at East 85th taking short leave of their places to waddle after an old man with a bag of bread crumbs. At West 100th—a road directly in the sun—several squirrels temporarily abandoned their positions to make umbrellas out of short sticks and leaves. And at West 86th, a mounted policeman jumped down from his horse and offered one drooping squirrel a shower from his canteen.

"Be careful!" Scruff called over. "That water might be contaminated! Accept no human hand-outs!" But Sally had in mind a handout of her own. She skated away and returned with three cans of soda, and straws, for the blockade line.

"I saw that!" Scruff cried. "Just what I need, Franklin—troops with stomach cramps! Ohh, that *clinging* girl! I don't see why you encouraged her to hang around this morning. I have enough to think about."

"Right you are," Franklin said, nodding to a crowd of reporters suddenly coming their way.

"Hey," one man said to Sally. "Aren't you the skateboard girl?"

Sally thought fast. The last thing she needed was her mother seeing her in the paper again.

"Uh . . . not me," she replied, and skateboard in tow, she walked quietly away.

Scruff watched her go. Good riddance, he thought.

50

"Look!" he heard a reporter shout. "There's the head squirrel!"

Scruff smiled. "Watch me charm the press," he whispered to Franklin. "Even though we're having some minor trouble in the ranks, we've got to keep up appearances. You know, seem calm and confident."

His eye cocked toward the reporters, Scruff dashed up a tree onto a low-hanging branch and began preening his tail.

"It's so difficult to decide whether my right or left side is more photogenic," he called down to Franklin as cameras began to click. "My manly brown tuft is more pronounced in my right profile, but my left better highlights my dark, brooding eyes."

"Hey, Scruff," the pigeon said, fluttering up to the squirrel's side. "It's fine to charm the press, but don't you think these pictures can wait? We need to find some backups."

The squirrel turned to the pigeon. "Franklin, positive media exposure is critical to our cause. Trust me. As soon as this little photo session is over, we'll get those troops." Just then a TV crew arrived. Scruff pushed a paw through his forelock and strutted farther out on the branch. "Now if you'll excuse me, my public awaits!"

A SHORT time later, Corker left the West 72nd line to complain to Mort.

51

"I had to take a break," he said. "That concrete is tough on the old legs."

The mouse grinned. "But your career as professional roadblock has only just begun. If you ache like this after a day, think how you'll feel in a year. You may well be the first squirrel ever to be placed in traction."

"I know," Corker replied. "A squirrel is put on this earth to prance, dash, pounce, and scamper, not stand day after day, paw to paw, on burning pavement. Or pose for pictures," he added, just as Scruff and Franklin, followed by reporters, appeared over the hill.

"I heard that," the squirrel snapped. "At least we're getting some publicity. That's what this uprising needs."

"What this uprising needs is more uprisers," Mort observed.

"Is that all anyone can talk about?" Scruff exclaimed. "I'm working on it."

"You are?" Mort said. "How?"

"Well . . . it's not so simple. . . . I'm just sure that, given time—"

A dark shape scurried across the grass. Scruff stiffened, sat up straight. He, Mort, Franklin, and Corker all sniffed. The unmistakable odor of rat! Seconds later, the intruder scuttled from the bushes alongside them.

"Hello, there, boys," he said.

Scruff and Mort recognized this rodent. His name was Grimbly, the leader of a local band of rats who lived in the bushes. He was a large brownish creature, with long greasy whiskers.

At the sight of him, the reporters headed hastily toward the park gate.

Scruff narrowed his eyes. "Well, well, Grimbly. What do you want?"

"Tsk, tsk, Scruffy, boy," the rat replied. "Don't look so peeved. It unbecomes you. I am here to offer assistance."

"Assistance?" Scruff snorted. "How could you possibly assist us?"

The rat chuckled. "Isn't it obvious? Word is, you want to take over the whole thing." Grimbly indicated the park with a sweep of his long, stringy tail. "To do that, you're going to need help. As you know, I am the charter president of the United Federation of Remarkable Rodents. We want a piece of the action."

Scruff shook himself. As far as he was concerned, rats were on the lowest rung of the evolutionary ladder, hovering somewhere around the cockroach and the human. But still, the offer had its appeal. There were millions of rats in New York.

"What's in it for you?" Scruff asked.

The rat grinned. "Merely the knowledge that we've helped a neighbor."

"Oh, give me a break," Mort scoffed.

Grimbly smiled at him. "Be quiet, my little reading friend, or I shall be forced to ingest you." He turned back to Scruff. "Of course, we wouldn't mind shutting off the park to humans, too."

"And their rat poison," Mort said.

The rat glared, showing sharp yellow teeth. "Desist, mouse! Obviously, if we were to help, we would need to be rewarded."

"Meaning what?" Scruff asked.

"In the interest of fairness, we would require sole control of the area of the park from Seventy-second Street south to Fifty-ninth."

Scruff's eyes snapped wide. "But some of the nicest parts of the whole thing are there! The Carousel, Wollman Rink, Tavern on the Green, and the Zoo—not to mention Sheep Meadow!"

Grimbly raised his eyebrows and smirked. "The choice is yours. It seems to me that without us you're finished. Before you know it, all your troops will be talking desertion. You see, fancy speeches don't matter for long when it's ninety-two degrees out."

Scruff cocked his head to the side. "Desertion!" he repeated. "Well ... hmmm. ... Maybe we could—"

"Good grief," Mort muttered. "Scruff, I never thought I'd see you listen to a rat."

Scruff shook himself. Mort was right. What *was*

he doing talking to Grimbly? It was beneath him—and not only that, bad for his reputation. Besides, using rats would give the mayor a perfect excuse to turn against them all. Humans hated rats even more than he did.

"Get lost," Scruff said. "And lay low, or else when we do have the park to ourselves, we might throw you out. Then it would be strictly basements and subways for you."

The rat sneered. "Okay, *Scruffy*. Have it your way. But when your whole operation falls apart, don't say we didn't try to help."

With a sweep of his tail, he disappeared into the bushes.

"He may be obnoxious," Franklin said, "but he's right."

"He sure is," Corker agreed. "I won't keep my troops here much longer without reinforcements. And without more grub!"

"I hear you, I hear you," Scruff chattered. "Just trust me, huh? Now, if you don't mind, get back to the line."

"All right. I'm going."

"And look cute," Scruff called after him. "Humans are suckers for *cute*."

On his way back to the West 72nd blockade, Corker loped by Sally in Strawberry Fields, gazing at the memorial to singer John Lennon, a stone medallion embedded in the pavement, bearing upon it the word *Imagine* in black letters. She seemed lost in thought.

A sparrow fluttered out of a nearby tree and glided gently to the edge of the park. She watched it go. The bird fluttered easily above the park wall, then spread its wings and soared out over Central Park West.

Sally turned her eyes again to the word *Imagine*. She took a deep breath of fresh air and then, her eyes bright, looked to where Scruff, Franklin, and Mort were still in conversation on the grass.

Suddenly, her heart jumped. She looked up and caught a final glimpse of the sparrow disappearing behind a building.

Birds . . .

She grabbed her skateboard and began running toward the animals.

Maybe it could work. . . .

"Hey, you guys!" she cried. "Listen up! I just thought of something!"

 # A Shock

SCRUFF shuddered.

"Easy does it now," Mort said. "Don't flip or anything."

"Me?" Scruff replied. "Flip?"

"Guess what?" Sally cried, pulling to a halt by the animals. "I've got an idea. A way for you to get help."

"Help? How does she know we need it?" He glared at Franklin and Mort. "No more notes, I hope!"

"Not from me," the pigeon replied. "But Scruff, Sally saw the situation this morning. She has eyes. She's a smart kid. And she believes in us. The least we can do is listen."

Sighing, Scruff sat. Franklin motioned to Sally to go on.

"Okay," she said, kneeling. "I was thinking about how beat some of the roadblockers looked earlier today. And then I saw this bird—a sparrow, I think—fly *out* of the park. Well, I got thinking: why not switch it around? Why not get birds from *outside* the park to come *in*? If the pigeons fly into the country, they could round up plenty of them. Probably thousands."

Scruff looked at Franklin and Mort wide-eyed. "What kind of plan is *that*?"

Franklin shrugged. "Sounds workable to me."

"Well, you're wrong!"

"Wrong? Why?"

Scruff exploded. "Because I've never heard anything stupider in my life. That's why! Outside the park? She suggests getting birds from *outside* the park?"

"That's right," Franklin said, fluttering about excitedly. "We pigeons fly off and spread the word, just like Sally said."

Scruff began ranting. "This is human idiocy at its most refined! Here I've been working like a maniac trying to hold this uprising together, and this girl waltzes in and says, 'Oh, don't worry, Scruff. Just get birds from outside the park. I'm sure they'd be glad to leave their nice little homes in the country and fly right down to help.' Next, I suppose she'll want you to take off for the South Pole and bring back a flock of penguins!"

"I don't think he likes the idea," Mort whispered to Franklin.

"Her plan is insane," Scruff raved. "No country bird would help us in a trillion years!" He wheeled around and faced the pigeon. "They *hate* the city. You know that, Franklin. How could you expect them willingly to defend our park?"

Franklin held still. Mort raised his eyebrows. "As much as I'm sorry to admit it, Franklin, the squirrel has a point."

"But Scruff," Sally cut in. She could tell by his chatters and hisses what the squirrel thought of her idea. "It could work! Imagine all the birds lined up along the stone wall around the park. It'll be easy to—"

Scruff's stomach clenched. This craziness had gone too far. So what if this girl had saved his life? Who cared if she had persuaded the Sheep Meadow squirrels to join by giving them skateboard rides? The uprising belonged to the animals. She had no business butting in.

"Animals like helping each other," Sally went on. "You'll see. Once I had a cat who really loved doing things for this dog in the apartment across from ours. Take it from me, Scruff—"

Take it from me? Was this girl giving him advice? Cats and dogs? What did they have to do with anything? He shivered.

"When the dog hurt his leg, the cat started licking the cut. You'll see."

Scruff blinked. You'll see? What was she doing anyway—trying to take over his uprising?

It was time, once and for all, to show this girl where she stood.

Scruff turned his back on Sally, dug his front paws into the dirt, and kicked savagely in her direction with his powerful hind legs. Clumps of dirt whipped into her face. She jumped up and covered her eyes as Scruff's legs continued pumping a mile a minute, like an out-of-control piece of machinery. Franklin and Mort were so shocked they didn't move.

"What are you doing?" Franklin exclaimed, once Scruff finally wound down. "Did it ever occur to you that Sally has feelings?"

"None that matter," Scruff snapped.

Franklin blinked. "None that *matter*?"

"You heard me! She's only a human, Franklin. It's time you realize that!" He spun around and cocked his legs toward Sally again.

"Enough!" Franklin cried, shielding Sally with his wings. "No more bullying!"

Scruff turned forward, and met the pigeon's eyes.

"They sure broke the mold when they made you, didn't they, Scruff? Everything has to be your way! *Your* idea! And if it's not, you stomp and rave and kick like a baby!"

"Sounds accurate to me," Mort said.

"Keep out of this!" the squirrel yelled.

Franklin fluttered his feathers. "You don't like humans because they litter and make noise. Yet you act worse than the worst of them! Good grief! Sally was only trying to help!"

"You call that plan *help*? She has no right—"

"Oh, be quiet." Franklin shook himself. "I'm tired of this whole business anyway. I hope every animal gives up. Taking over Central Park? I was a fool to have gotten involved in the first place. I'm out of here."

Sally watched breathlessly as her friend lifted off and flew out of the park.

"Do me a favor," Franklin called down to Mort. "Please say good-bye to Sally for me."

"What?"

"Tear her a message. Tell her thanks for everything."

"Coward!" Scruff cried toward the sky. "Go ahead! Desert at our moment of greatest need!"

But Franklin didn't look back.

Scruff turned to Mort. "The nerve of that bird!"

"I guess he just got fed up," the mouse observed.

"Fed up?" Scruff replied. "I'm the one who should be fed up. From the very beginning, Franklin has involved that girl in everything." He scowled at Sally. "By the way, Mort, I trust you aren't going to get her that good-bye note?"

Mort shrugged. "The way I figure it, it'll be the last time I'll have to rip papers for anyone. So why not?"

Scruff crept closer. "Because that girl has caused enough damage for one lifetime, that's why. If not for her stupid idea, Franklin would still be with us! No animal is ever going to talk to her again. Not if I can help it!"

"Oh, give me a break," Mort said, turning toward his hole. "The girl hasn't been your problem."

With a giant leap, Scruff was in front of him, up on his haunches, his paw cocked. His dark eyes glinted menacingly.

Frightened, Sally drew back.

"My dear mouse, if you so much as go near a piece of newspaper in the next five minutes, I'll—"

Mort's whiskers twitched. "Easy does it, Scruff. Relax."

"Relax?" Scruff's black eyes were dancing. "Oh, I'm as calm as a kitten. But I mean what I say. No more notes! Do you hear?"

The squirrel feinted with his paw. Mort shuffled backwards.

"All right, all right. I hear." A safe distance away, the mouse stopped. "But before I go, tell me something. If you aren't willing to at least try Sally's plan, where *are* you going to get more recruits?"

The squirrel waved his right paw. "Oh, I've millions of untapped sources. Why, I could dredge up another hundred or more from around the reservoir with a single word."

"The reservoir?" Mort shook his head. "Hey, if you can make yourself believe that, more power to you." He sighed and looked at Sally. "Oh, well, I suppose she'll figure out what's happened without a message. See you, Scruff."

"Bye, bye, *Morty*."

As the mouse disappeared behind a bench, Scruff rose on his haunches to face Sally.

"Enjoy the park while you can, little girl!" he said. "Because when it's mine, just try and get in. *Just try!* I'll tie you to that silly skateboard and catapult you over Fifth Avenue!"

Scruff turned and bounded over the hill.

Heart pounding, Sally took deep breaths. Everything had gone wrong—*and all because of her plan!* And worse, it was clear that Franklin had left the uprising.

Somehow, she knew it was for good. But she couldn't stop herself from looking up, hoping to see the pigeon swoop down again from the sky.

It was then that she felt a light touch on her shoulder. She turned and saw a young police officer with a handlebar mustache.

"Hiya," he said, holding out his hand. "I'm Officer Maurice Greene."

"Hi," Sally said, taking his hand for a second.

"You're the skateboard girl, aren't you?"

Sally nodded. She didn't have the energy to deny it.

The officer looked around. "Where're your little friends?"

How could she admit to a policeman what had happened?

"Out rounding up more troops, I guess."

"More troops, eh?" Officer Greene asked, squatting next to her. "So what do you think they'll do next? Take over the whole city?"

Sally forced a smile. "Maybe. . . . Then maybe one of them'll run for mayor."

Officer Greene laughed. "I wouldn't be surprised. Well, have a nice evening."

Sally watched Officer Greene walk across the

street back to the roadblock. Then she grabbed her skateboard and, too preoccupied to see where she was going, ran smack into a man lugging a cello case into the park.

"Sorry!"

She sprinted all the way home, fighting back tears.

"DEAR?" Mrs. March asked Sally that evening. "Are you all right? You haven't touched your supper."

Sally nodded, slowly. "I'm okay, Mom."

"You don't sound okay. What happened in the park?"

Sally wanted to tell her but couldn't find the words.

"You'll feel better if you talk it out."

Sally sighed. "Well," she said at last, "I suggested getting birds from outside the park. But Scruff got mad . . . and then Franklin left."

"Left? For good?"

"I think so . . . and without him, I'm afraid the uprising'll be over."

Sally's mother nodded sympathetically.

"You know," she said, softly, "it has to end sometime. Isn't it better that it's sooner rather than later, before any of the squirrels get hurt?"

Sally forced a nod. "Yes. I guess so."

"Anyway," her mother said. "Thank goodness those squirrels haven't blocked the pedestrian paths."

"Why?"

"The New York Philharmonic is playing a concert tonight at the Great Lawn."

"You mean in the park—Central Park?"

"Uhm-hmm. I thought it might be canceled because of the animals. But I heard on the radio that the orchestra members will bring in their equipment on foot. I'm meeting your father there in an hour. Now eat up. Your sitter will be here soon."

Suddenly, the image of Franklin swaying gently to the radio flashed through Sally's mind.

"What pieces are they playing?"

"Mozart's Fortieth Symphony, Brahms's Third, and Gershwin's *An American in Paris*."

Sally gasped. Wasn't it Mozart that Franklin had been listening to on the radio?

"Wait," Sally said. "Is it too late to cancel the sitter?"

Mrs. March looked surprised. "Why, I suppose not. . . ."

Sally jumped up from the table.

"Where're you going?"

"To the park. Please, Mom?"

Mrs. March sighed. "I'm willing to bet that this

sudden interest in classical music has more to do with those squirrels than with Mozart or Brahms. But okay. Meet us in front of the Delacorte Theater at Seventy-ninth Street at seven sharp."

"COME *on*," Sally said, leaning over Mort's hole behind the park bench minutes later. "I know you're in there."

She waited.

"I'm not leaving till you come out, Morty!"

"Good grief!" Mort moaned. "Can't a poor mouse read in peace?"

He emerged to look right into Sally's expectant face.

"Oh, good," she began. "Now, I know you can't talk to me, but listen. We can't let the uprising end. It's come too far. It's too exciting. So I've got to convince Franklin to fly for country birds. He's the only one who can. I'm sure he'll be at the Philharmonic concert tonight, because the other day he was listening to classical music in my room. I know he loves it. So I need you to come with me to translate, and please don't say no, Morty! Please!"

"The name is *Mort*!" the mouse squeaked.

"Please!" Sally repeated.

Mort sighed, then nodded. There was something about the girl. . . .

"My intellect has become my curse!" he grumbled, but scuttled forward onto Sally's open palms.

She could hardly contain her excitement. Imagine! A mouse in her hands, perhaps even the success of the whole uprising!

At the Great Lawn

THE Great Lawn was jammed with people on blankets, eating picnic suppers and waiting for the concert to begin.

Sally, her eyes peeled for Franklin, paid the crowd little attention. But the only bird she'd seen resembling her friend was an off-white warbler perched on the top of the Delacorte Theater.

By the time her family found a spot—about four city blocks from the stage—the musicians were already tuning up.

"I brought over some cake for dessert," Mrs. March told Sally.

"Say," her father said as they spread out their blanket, "what's that moving under your shirt?"

"What do you mean, Dad?"

"I thought I saw something rustle."

"Um . . . it's a secret. For later."

If she doesn't let me out soon, Mort thought, I'll be one squashed mouse. Being cramped like this is tough on precious brain cells.

Sally craned her neck. She suspected Franklin would be near the orchestra, but she could hardly see the stage for all the people.

"Look, dear," Mrs. March exclaimed, pointing toward a man in a tuxedo striding into view. "That's the conductor."

The crowd hushed. Up above, Sally could make out three dim stars. The conductor waved his baton and the music began—*An American in Paris* by George Gershwin. Sally was surprised at how much she liked it but resisted listening too carefully. She had work to do.

Her first problem was how to slip away. Should she wait for a break, or should she make some excuse and go now?

Before she could decide, Mort made the decision for her. She felt an intense scrambling under her shirt, and the next moment he was skittering across their blanket. Mrs. March screamed. Hundreds of angry eyes turned their way. Terrified, the mouse dashed through the field of people.

"Morty!" Sally cried.

"Sally!" her mother gasped. "Come back here!"

But Sally was already jumping over blankets and picnic baskets, not to mention people.

"You stay here," Mr. March said to his wife, starting after Sally. "I'll take care of this."

Mort was heading toward the stage. Sally could easily follow his route by listening to screams and seeing people leap up or slap at their blankets.

"Hey!" a woman cried. "This is a concert! Have a little respect!"

Two policemen hustled near. The orchestra played an upbeat rhythm as though the music had been chosen to accompany the chase.

"Watch it!" a man bellowed, as Sally accidentally kicked his cheesecake.

"Sorry!" Sally said.

"My Lord!" another man blurted. "First those animals block the roads, and now this!"

"Sally!" her father yelled. "Stop this instant!"

But she had to keep running. If anything happened to that mouse, she'd feel horrible. Not only could Mort be stepped on and hurt; but if he got away, she'd lose her one means of communicating with Franklin and saving the uprising. Just then, she saw a man stomp on a blanket with his boots.

"Oh, no!" she cried.

To her relief, she heard another scream closer to the stage. Mort was still alive and running!

And how he ran, barreling through the crowd, steering clear of feet, hands, pans, and plates.

Why me? he thought, breathless. And just when I was up to President Warren G. Harding in my trivia book—one of the best tuba players ever to reach the White House!

He rushed closer and closer to the stage. More police followed, and more people swatted. Mort dodged a cookie tray. He swerved around a trash can. But then his luck ran out. A man stood up, cocked his leg . . .

"Morty!" Sally cried.

Boom! Mort flipped through the air and landed directly on the conductor's head.

"What is this?" the conductor screamed.

Mort hung on for dear life. The man grabbed at his head and did what looked like a tribal rain dance. The orchestra, following his lead, picked up the tempo. Mort dropped to the floor as four policemen rushed onto the stage.

"Morty!" Sally cried again.

Just then a white shape whipped past her ear.

"It's the pigeon!" someone yelled.

Sally's eyes lit up.

"Franklin!"

The next thing she knew, he had swooped onto the stage, grabbed Mort's tail in his beak, and flown off. By now, Sally's father had caught up with her.

"Sally," he panted. "What on earth are you doing?"

"Dad," she cried, pointing. "There's Franklin!"

Mr. March looked up just in time to see the pigeon disappear behind the stage.

"I've got to talk to him."

"No. You're coming back with me, and we're going home."

"Dad! I have to! Please! Everything depends on it!"

BEHIND the stage, Mort was huddled in a ball, frantically licking his tail.

"What were you trying to do, you crazy bird? Rip me apart?"

"I was saving you from certain death," Franklin replied.

"Oh, really? Next time, grab me by the back of the neck or something. My tail is very sensitive."

"What're you doing here, anyway?" Franklin asked. "I came to listen in peace to some of my favorite compositions. You're a bookworm, not a music mouse."

"It's not me," Mort said. "It's that girl. She conned me into helping."

Almost before Franklin could react to this news, Sally appeared out of the shadows.

"I'll keep an eye on you from here," Mr. March said from behind her. "Try not to be too long. Your mother will be frantic."

Sally stepped forward and knelt.

"See?" Mort said. "I told you."

"Franklin!" Sally said. "And Morty! Are you okay?"

"No, I'm not okay!" the mouse began. "And, I repeat, the name is Mort. Not Morty! Mort. M−O−R−T. Aw, what's the use? She can't understand me anyway."

The pigeon scratched anxiously at his feathers.

"It's good to see you, Franklin," Sally said. "Listen . . . I have to hurry. But I came to tell you something. You've got to help the uprising."

Franklin froze on one foot, his eyes wide.

"She can't see it's over," Mort said.

"You've come *so* far," Sally continued. "You can't just let it fall apart. You and your friends could fly off tonight and try to convince some of those country birds to help."

Franklin cocked his head. "Hey, Mort," he said. "Could you do me a favor?"

"Does it involve reading?"

"Of course."

"I figured. Hold on."

Mort disappeared beneath the stage. Knowing he was off to find a newspaper, Sally sat still. Above her, she heard the final saxophone wail of *An American in Paris*, and then a roar of applause. A second later, Mort appeared dragging the *Daily News*.

"Tell her I've decided Scruff is crazy," Franklin said.

"How am I supposed to tell her that?"

"How should I know? You're the one who's so smart."

Mort flipped to page two and began reading. Sally looked over her shoulder at her father. She wished the mouse would hurry.

"I can find 'the uprising' and 'head squirrel' but that's it."

"That's plenty," Franklin said. "Could you rip them out? It's hard to do with my claws."

Mort did, and seconds later the pigeon took the first scrap of paper in his beak and hovered in front of Sally.

" 'The head squirrel,' " Sally read. "Yes?"

Franklin let the paper drop to the ground; then he began rolling his eyes and flying in short, tight circles, flapping his wings.

"What?" Sally said. Then Franklin's meaning

hit her. "Okay, okay," she said. "You can stop that. I know Scruff is crazy. That's not the point."

Franklin sighed. "Mort, give me the other piece of paper."

The pigeon dropped it in front of Sally.

" 'The uprising,' " Sally read. "Okay. What about it?"

As Sally watched, Franklin began ripping the piece of paper into little bits. He dug his claws in and shredded it until there was next to nothing left.

"That says it for sure," Mort snickered.

Sally's heart leaped. "Aw, come on, Franklin! You can't mean that! You can't quit! I don't care if Scruff is the craziest animal in the world. What he *wants* is right. The park is *your* home. Don't you see? You can't stop now before you've gotten anything out of it! If you can talk the country birds into coming and taking over the whole park, think what that'll mean! You'll finally get a little attention!"

"Keep your voice down, dear," her father said. "You're shouting."

"Dad. This is important! Don't just sit there, Franklin! Go on! Get flying before the troops desert! Get those country birds! It's our last chance!"

Franklin bobbed his head back and forth. Maybe the girl had a point. . . . It would be a pity to see it all crumble now. And if they were successful, even for a short time, maybe the humans would treat them better.

As the orchestra played the opening phrase of Mozart's Fortieth, Franklin brushed his wing against Sally's knee, then circled up into the sky.

"Hey!" Mort shouted. "You aren't going to help?"

But the pigeon was gone, his white body swallowed up in the darkness.

Sally, understanding, whooped for joy.

Birdmania

As Franklin soared into the night, the stirring strains of the Philharmonic drifted across the park to the West 72nd Street roadblock. Scruff sat glumly in his tree, tired and discouraged that he had found no more squirrels at the reservoir. Maybe Grimbly was right; maybe he would be reduced to using rats after all.

"Curse that music!" he cried, covering his ears with his paws. "Can't a general get some sleep?"

But when sleep finally came, Scruff tossed and turned all night and was plagued by nightmares.

Strapped to the back of a high-flying pigeon, he dreamed he was soaring above the outer boroughs of the city—the Bronx, Queens, Brooklyn, Staten Island—searching, searching. . . .

"You, down there," he heard himself call to squirrel after squirrel. "And you! Hurry! You're my last hope!"

But Scruff in his dream met with failure after failure. One group of squirrels successfully sneaked onto the Staten Island Ferry but were stopped at the New York docks when they couldn't come up with their twenty-five-cent fares. A troop from the Bronx took the subway as far as Times Square but were finally chased down by transit police. And about two hundred squirrels from the Brooklyn Botanical Gardens dashed under the turnstiles and onto a train only to discover they were going in the wrong direction. From atop his pigeon, Scruff found them on the Coney Island boardwalk asking directions from a sea gull.

"This way!" he cried. "Follow me! Hurry! There's no time to lose!"

But the squirrels didn't hear, and Scruff reeled into yet another nightmare.

Perched on a throne at West 72nd Street, a

crown on his head, he was King Scruff, mighty ruler of Central Park.

"Ah, yes!" he exclaimed. "I do feel fine!"

Then, in the distance, he saw Sally, skateboarding out of the park.

"Excellent!" he cried, standing on his hind legs. "That sniveling human is finally going home where she belongs!"

But then his body went rigid.

Behind Sally, on skateboards of their own, were Franklin and Mort. And behind *them*, also skateboarding, was a line of squirrels and pigeons—two miles long!

Scruff tore across the pavement.

"Hey, there!" he cried. "Get back to your blockade! Immediately! All of you!"

But Franklin and Mort smiled placidly in his direction.

"We're going to live at Sally's house," they said.

"You're what?" Scruff shrieked. His crown fell to the pavement.

"We're going to live at Sally's house!"

"No, you're not!" Scruff cried wildly, racing up and down the line of skateboarding animals. "What about the uprising? Stop, I say! Stop!"

But the procession moved faster, and the chanting grew louder and louder. Scruff threw himself on the pavement, sobbed, kicked the cement with his paws.

"No! You can't! Don't leave me! Please! *Please!!*"

"Hey, Scruff!"

He woke with a start, his chest heaving, his fur matted with tears. Shielding his eyes against the early morning light, he peered down the tree.

Just what he needed—the skateboard girl!

"I know what you think of me," she called up. "But just look. Look!"

Over the rim of the east side of the park, Scruff heard a faint fluttering, like the low distant rumble of a train, followed by the shouts of many voices:

"Will you look at that!"

"What is it?"

"It's a black mass—a tornado!"

"It's a swarm of locusts!"

Scruff spun around.

"No!" he heard a policeman yell. "It's birds! Hundreds and hundreds of birds! Thousands!"

The squirrel shook himself. Was he still dreaming? He stood still, too amazed to react as the cloud of birds, first a speck on the horizon, grew larger and larger until, slowly but surely, it overtook the skyline.

The reinforcements were crossing the East River now. Caws, chirps, and cackles filled the air as they thundered closer. Scruff followed their flight across the city. First Avenue, now Second Avenue, now Third . . . Lexington . . . Park . . . Madison . . . Fifth.

When they reached the east side of the park, Scruff squinted. He couldn't believe it! His heart jumped. At the front of the pack was a white pigeon!

Seconds later, Franklin soared overhead and landed on the branch next to Scruff.

"We would've been here sooner," the pigeon gasped, "but we got held up dodging planes at La Guardia Airport."

Scruff craned his neck and laughed. He had to admit it, the birds were an inspiring sight. They hovered above the lower west side of the park now, casting a gigantic shadow. The wind from the wings washed Sally's body with a cool breeze.

"It's good to see you, Franklin," Scruff said.

"Yes, well . . . where should I direct the birds?"

"The wall surrounding the park!" the squirrel cried. "This is our big moment! We'll block off everything at one time!"

Franklin took to the air. Scruff bounded out of his tree, up to West 72nd Street.

"Greet our friends the country birds!" he cried as squirrels who had deserted began pointing and jabbering and hustling back into line. "Here in the city to assist us in our noble cause!"

Sally ran to the edge of the park just as the first group of birds came in for a triumphant landing on the wall.

There were robins, blue jays, blackbirds, warblers, woodpeckers, orioles, and many others she couldn't possibly name. There was a large bird with a long S-shaped neck. A pelican perhaps? There was a pink bird with elegant, sticklike legs—a flamingo?

She felt a light weight on her shoulder.

"Franklin!"

Sally saw shadows under his eyes. No doubt he had been up all night. But despite his exhaustion, he radiated happiness.

She opened her hand, expecting a note to drop into her palm. Instead, Franklin cooed musically and flew off to Scruff's tree. Sally smiled, thrilled, again, that she had been able to convince the pigeon to give it one last try.

"Hmm. . . . Looks like your friends got a little help," observed Maurice Greene, the young policeman with the handlebar mustache, as a group of wrens and sapsuckers settled on a wall a bit uptown. "If those birds keep coming, it shouldn't take them more than twenty-four hours to block off the whole thing. Maybe less."

Sally followed a flight of sparrows and cardinals angling toward the south side of the park. "Yep," she said happily. "It looks that way."

Back at his tree, Scruff gazed east, where a black line of birds stretched across the horizon.

"How beautiful they look, Franklin!" he cried. "How utterly gorgeous!" He clapped his paws de-

83

lightedly. "And to think it all started with an idea I had, what was it, only four . . . no, five days ago!" He breathed deeply. "Then we were nothing! Now we rule!"

Franklin looked at Scruff. Despite all that had happened, he couldn't help feeling good for the squirrel.

"It *is* quite a sight," the pigeon agreed, watching Scamp direct a line of orioles onto the wall to the left.

"Quite a sight?" Scruff asked. He stood full up on his back legs and waved his paws broadly. "This is history, Franklin, my friend! Mort reads about it, but we're living it! We're the George Washington and Thomas Jefferson of a new land—a land of the animals, run by the animals, for the animals!" His dark eyes shone. His dream seemed so close he could taste it. "What a day to be alive!" he exclaimed. "Oh, what a *glorious* day to be a squirrel!"

NEWS of the birds spread quickly. Network anchormen interrupted TV shows to keep Americans up-to-date.

"We're talking birds, ladies and gentlemen," a reporter announced from the scene. "Hundreds of them! No one knows why they're here, but what is undeniably clear is that they have turned New York City into a naturalist's dream."

84

By ten o'clock, the State Parks Department proclaimed Manhattan an animal sanctuary, and environmentalists gathered from all over. A well-known ornithologist, famous for his research on flamingo sleeping patterns, jetted in from Florida.

"There are enough species at just the East One hundred second Street wall to fill ten books!" he exulted.

As they had done with squirrels earlier in the week, New Yorkers became obsessed with birds. The Audubon Society signed up three thousand new members by eleven o'clock. The Museum of Natural History hastily mounted an exhibit on North American park birds to complement their show on squirrel evolution.

Bird business boomed. Soon, every parrot or parakeet in the city had been bought. Birdseed, down pillows, birdbaths, bird whistles, birdcages, posters of the Birdman of Alcatraz, discs of the jazz standard "Birdland," and basketball player Larry Bird's biography were sold out of every store.

The leader of the punk rock band The Squirrel Heads got to work on a new song, "Oh, My Wordy! Here Comes the Birdy!"

But some residents weren't so pleased with the new arrivals.

"When it was just pigeons and squirrels, I thought it was kind of cute," a hot dog vendor at West 72nd complained to a customer late that morning. "But when every bird on the East Coast starts showing up, that's where I draw the line. These animals are playing for keeps!"

"This squawking is worse than Chinese water torture," a woman told a reporter as she ate her lunch near a line of birds at Columbus Circle. "And wouldn't you know it? Every store is fresh out of earplugs!"

Officer Maurice Greene was found early that afternoon at a drinking fountain, washing a white splotch off his cap.

"Hey," a boy asked with a grin. "Get hit?"

Officer Greene glanced briefly overhead and shook his head. "I tell you," he said, forcing a smile. "As long as these birds are around, it's going to be awfully hard to keep a clean uniform."

As the day passed, word of the uprising continued to spread among country birds, all the way from the suburbs of Connecticut to the pastures of Vermont. In Upstate New York, a black crow was chewing on a cornstalk when his cousin landed next to him.

"Hey, Mo," the second crow cried.

"Hiya, Gil," Mo cawed back, the cornstalk still in his beak. "What's new?"

"A whole buncha birds have been takin' off for New York!"

Mo stopped midchew.

"You mean New York City?"

"Yep."

"What for?"

"Somethin' about a bunch of squirrels," Gil replied. "What do ya say we check it out?"

"You mean go to *New York*?"

"That's right. All work and no play makes Mo a dull crow. This is a chance for a little adventure. I've never been to a city, and neither have you. Let's live a little."

Mo finished the stalk he'd been working on.

"Well," he said with a shrug. "Just as long as we're back here by the day after tomorrow for the cornhuskin' fair."

The two crows took to the air and headed south.

"I expect it'll be crowded there," Mo cawed.

"Yep," Gil agreed with a nod. "More crowded than a barrel full of hogs at a tractor pull."

By the time Mo and Gil arrived in the city, more than half the walls had been blocked off. Birdcalls rang through the late afternoon air like trumpets.

"So here we are," Mo said as they squeezed their way into the mass of feathers on a wall by West 95th Street. Before them, a line of people had gathered to stare at and size up the new visitors. "Wow, but this place is a sight."

"It surely is," Gil agreed.

"Hey," Mo went on, gesturing toward the crowd with his wing. "Why do you suppose that fellow over there is holdin' his hands to his ears?"

"Ya got me," Gil replied. "Maybe it's some new fashion."

"I believe he objects to our squeaks and squawks," a well-groomed robin next to them remarked.

"Squeaks and squawks?" a nearby raven exclaimed. "But we aren't being loud."

"It may not seem so to you," the robin replied. "But to human ears, it's a different story. Though the city has a reputation for noise, the area around Central Park is usually quiet."

"Oh," Mo said. "So you've been here before?"

"I should say," the robin replied haughtily. "This city is a cultural mecca. Though I reside in the suburbs, it just so happens that my nest is in a tree in the backyard of a member of the Metropolitan Opera! Naturally, I fly over three times each summer to hear her sing in the free Opera in the Park. It's a delight. Her vocal capacity is extraordinary. She's a coloratura."

"A colora-what?" Mo said.

"A coloratura," the robin repeated. "A soprano with a light, airy vocal texture."

Mo and Gil exchanged a glance.

"Jiminy," Gil muttered. "We're gonna meet all types here. All types."

. . .

" 'BIRD madness sweeps Manhattan,' " the mayor read aloud to his aides that night. "The *Daily News* says, 'No one knows what animals will do next. . . . Appointments with mental health professionals triple. . . . Caws, coos, and cackles reach record decibel levels. . . . Heat wave bakes greater metropolitan area. . . . Citizens clamor for action from City Hall. . . .' "

He threw the paper across the room and began to pace.

"What should I do?" he moaned. "If I use force against this uprising, I'll be compared to Genghis Khan! I can just see the headline: FOWL PLAY! BIRD-BRAINED MAYOR SLAUGHTERS INNOCENT VISITORS!"

"It is a tricky situation, sir," his deputy agreed. "At this rate, the park'll be completely blocked off in a few hours. Then no humans will get in."

"No humans?"

The mayor slumped in his chair. His deputy reached for a tray in the middle of the desk and held a jelly doughnut in the air. Despite his worries, the mayor smiled.

"Ah, yes!" he said. "Blueberry filled. So sweet! Nothing like its delicate blend of dough, sugar, and jelly to calm the nerves and delight the senses. Highly yummy!"

The doughnut quickly disappeared. The mayor took three deep breaths.

"You know," the police chief began, once the mayor had collected himself enough to continue. "You could contact the skateboard girl. We had word that she was at the concert last night creating a disturbance with a mouse and the white pigeon. She might be a useful connection with the animals."

The mayor swung his legs up onto his desk. "Hmm," he said. "She could help. But how would it look to ask a girl to do my work?"

"Maybe not as bad as you think," his deputy said. "In fact, it might make you look good."

"Really?"

"There comes a time in a great leader's career when he needs to make a daring decision. We can present it to the press that way."

The parks commissioner brushed a hand through her hair. "That's right," she agreed. "The papers'll love it. I can see the headlines: MAYOR ASKS CHILD TO SAVE CITY!"

That wouldn't be bad, the mayor figured.

"In any case, it doesn't look like we have much choice," his deputy continued. "We want to end this uprising peacefully, right? It'll be hard to do that without some sort of contact with the animals themselves."

"I agree," the police chief said with a quick nod. "If the birds succeed in blocking out the people, there'll be chaos in the streets. People need to get into Central Park. They'll demand it."

The mayor sighed and glanced at his watch. "Well, it's nine-forty. This skateboard girl is probably asleep. Let's find out her name, and I'll get in touch first thing in the morning." His aides stood up and headed for the door. "And someone make sure that we have an ample supply of you-know-whats for tomorrow. You can't expect me to perform up to full capacity under pressure conditions without plenty of doughnuts!"

Fluttering Feathers, Bushy Tails, Glinting Eyes

"SALLY!" Mr. March said, awakening his daughter early on Friday. "You'd better get up."

Sally stretched. "Why?"

"The mayor wants to see you."

MINUTES later, she was sitting next to her father in the backseat of a limousine.

"Are birds still showing up?" she asked the driver as the big black car pulled away from the curb.

"Nope. The head squirrel was seen guiding the last of them onto a wall by the Metropolitan Museum around midnight."

"Then the whole thing's blocked off?"

"Sure is. All the way up to One hundred tenth Street from the west side to the east. See for yourself."

As the limo turned uptown onto Central Park West, Sally pressed her head to the window and gripped her skateboard. Central Park rose magically before her, its tall trees shrouded by morning mist. Pressed up against a sturdy row of police, swarms of people lined the streets, mouths agape, pointing, shaking their heads, unable to believe their eyes.

Sally could hardly believe hers: perched peacefully on the stone wall that surrounds the park, stretched uptown and downtown as far as she could see, was a perfect line of country birds— rank upon rank of them—and, still blocking the roads themselves, row upon row of squirrels and pigeons.

"Are there any people at all inside?" Mr. March asked.

"None that we know of. Around five this morning, packs of squirrels chased out the few humans who were left."

Sally's heart was pounding wildly. "They actually did it," she whispered to herself as they motored uptown past an unending line of fluttering feathers, bushy tails, and glinting eyes. "They've blocked every inch!"

If it weren't for a siren hastily attached to the roof, the trip up Central Park West and across 110th Street to the east side would've been slowgoing. But only minutes later, the limo pulled into the driveway of a huge white house.

"Gracie Mansion," Mr. March whispered. "The mayor's home."

Sally nodded. A policeman waved the car through a gate. Soon Sally and her father were being led down a wide hall, past a secretary's desk, and into an office.

The mayor and his chief aides were seated at a conference table.

"Hello, Sally," he said, standing up. "Welcome! And you must be Sally's father, Mr. March. So sorry to get you out this early, but I'm sure you understand. We have a bit of a problem in the park. Please! Sit, sit. Have a doughnut. Have two! That's it. Help yourself. No! No! Not the chocolate glazed. That's my favorite. Sorry. And the cinnamon filled is for my deputy. That's right. There you are. Plain doughnuts aren't so bad, are they? Now, meet the rest of the crew: the deputy mayor, the parks commissioner, and the chief of police."

Sally and her father shook hands all around the room.

"Whoa!" the mayor said, sounding suddenly alarmed. "Who took the maple walnut?"

The parks commissioner looked up sheepishly. "I thought you were having chocolate glazed," she said.

"I am," the mayor exclaimed. "For an appetizer! Maple walnut is my dessert."

The commissioner slipped her doughnut back onto the tray.

"Now," the mayor continued, turning to Sally, "we've had our breakfast. Let us begin, shall we?"

The mayor paused to collect his thoughts. In his long political career, he had asked many people to do many chores and favors, but never in his memory had he asked a ten-year-old girl to act as a go-between with a group of roadblocking squirrels.

"So . . . Sally . . . from the beginning of the animals' little uprising, there have been numerous reports as to your involvement, especially with the two ringleaders."

"You mean Scruff and Franklin?"

The mayor and his commissioners exchanged glances.

"Are those the names of the head squirrel and the white pigeon?" the parks commissioner asked.

Sally nodded.

"How do you know?"

"Morty showed me."

"Morty?"

"I believe he's a mouse," Sally's father said. "A mouse who can read and rips messages out of the newspaper. That's how they communicate with Sally."

The mayor shut his eyes for a minute and visualized his opponent in the November election ridiculing him on citywide television.

"I think I need that maple walnut," he said. He took a bite and walked to the window. "The girl's a lunatic," he muttered to himself.

But what if she isn't?

"Sally," he said, turning back. "You're an intelligent girl. Tell me, do you think you could get this squirrel—Scruff, I think you said—to call off the uprising? After all, he's had four days of it."

Sally whispered, "Call it off, sir?"

"That's right." The mayor resumed his seat. "Now, I know Scruff must have his reasons for taking over the park. But Sally, it's supposed to be ninety-three degrees today, and humid. And tomorrow, they say it's going up to ninety-five! You can't expect people to stay out of the park. So speak to the squirrel, won't you? Tell him he's had his laughs, but enough is enough."

Sally couldn't think of what to say. She knew

enough about Scruff to know that the uprising had never been for laughs.

"You see," Mr. March spoke up, "Sally has grown quite close to the animals."

"Close?" the mayor said. "I understand. A child's friendship with an animal is sacred. Nothing brings tears to the eye quicker than the sight of a little boy throwing a stick to his faithful dog." The mayor rose from his chair. "But Sally, if you do care about these animals, *that's all the more reason to help*. I don't want to see Central Park littered by thousands of trampled birds and squirrels any more than you. But unless you assist us, it could happen. I'm sure you saw the crowds lined up around the park. The police may not be able to hold them back much longer."

There was a heavy silence. The mayor sank once again into his seat. A thick lump rose in Sally's throat. Though she was honored to be asked to do something so important for the city, she couldn't bear the thought of the uprising coming to an end. Especially when the animals had only just accomplished their true goal. But the mayor's words echoed through her mind. What if the crowds *did* storm the park? She imagined the animals fleeing in panic, or, worse, hurt or trampled underfoot. She had certainly never bargained for that.

Sally glanced at her father. He gave her hand a squeeze. Then she drew a deep breath and looked up at a table of expectant faces.

"I'll do my best," she said, softly.

The mayor stood up. "Then it's settled."

"But there's one thing you should know," Sally went on.

"Yes?"

"It's about Scruff."

"What about him?" the deputy asked.

Sally sighed. "I'm not his friend at all. He doesn't like me very much."

The mayor and his commissioners shifted in their chairs.

"But I thought—" the police chief began.

"Oh, I'm good friends with Franklin, and Mort likes me well enough. But Scruff . . ." Sally shook her head. "He's a tough character. One of the last times I saw him, he kicked dirt in my face."

The mayor rubbed his chin. "I think I understand. That is upsetting. But Sally, you're the only one in the city who has any kind of relationship with him at all. And if the pigeon and mouse are there, perhaps they'll listen."

Sally nodded. "I guess that's true."

"No one's going to blame you if the squirrel refuses to talk," the deputy said.

"That's right," the parks commissioner added. "Just do your best."

Sally considered, then looked to the mayor and nodded.

"Let's get going," he said.

THE day was already heating up as Sally, her father, and the mayor pulled into West 72nd Street. News of their arrival had preceded them; a whole squad of police was needed to restrain the swelling crowd, a crowd that seemed to be doubling by the minute. The Squirrel Heads were on hand, signing autographs and posing for pictures. Gripping her skateboard, Sally followed the mayor across the pavement.

"I'm sick and tired of coddling these animals," she heard a woman tell a reporter. "What about *my* rights?"

"A steamroller would end this thing in a hurry," a man observed.

"Hey! Get your HEAD SQUIRREL FOR PRESIDENT T-shirts here!" a vendor called.

Sally grabbed her father's hand tightly as they made their way toward the stone entrance gates of the park.

"Sally!" her mother called from the back of the crowd.

"Let her through!" the mayor commanded.

"The deputy mayor phoned and told me you'd be here," Mrs. March said, kissing Sally on the cheek.

"Mr. Mayor!" a reporter shouted. "Are you really sending a girl into the park to talk to the squirrels?"

The onlookers hushed. The mayor's bald spot turned red. He suddenly craved another maple walnut doughnut.

"Yes, I am!" he declared finally.

Murmurs rippled through the crowd.

"My opponent says I lack the imagination to lead effectively," he continued. "Well, if relying on Sally here doesn't show imagination, I don't know what does."

"But do you think the squirrels'll listen to her?"

All eyes turned toward the roadblock. Pigeons and squirrels stood six rows deep. At the front were Franklin, Mort, Corker, Ripper, and Scamp. And in the middle was the head squirrel himself, perched squarely on all fours, his tail perked, his brown forelock of hair blowing in the hot breeze. Sally and the mayor exchanged a troubled look.

"Absolutely!" the mayor declared.

He nodded in Sally's direction. Her legs felt weak in the hot sun. Bravely, she hugged her father, kissed her mother, and turned toward the blockade. Reporters murmured. Cameras hummed and clicked. The crowd pushed forward and hushed. Sally took a small step.

But then, Scruff rose to his back legs and scowled threateningly.

The crowd gasped. Heart pounding, Sally stopped dead in her tracks. Who was she kidding? The hard glint in the squirrel's eyes told the story. He would never talk to her! He'd snub her in front of the entire city!

"What'samatta, skateboard girl?" a teenager cried. "Scared or somethin'?"

Sally shot him a glance.

"Oh, boy!" she heard a reporter cry. "That squirrel looks ready to take on the whole city single-handedly!"

"Go for it, Sally!"

She looked behind her. There was Officer Maurice Greene, giving the thumbs-up sign. Nearby, the mayor leaned forward, pleadingly. And then there was the crowd.

"Hurry it up, skateboard girl!" a man cried. "I've got an eight-thirty breakfast meeting!"

Sally trembled. The people of New York had had enough—she knew it. She must try to talk to Scruff, like it or not. If she didn't, it was certain the crowd and police would take matters into their own hands.

She turned back to the blockade and took a deep breath. A bead of sweat dripped down her back. Determined now, she took ten resolute steps

to the line of animals, knelt, and placed her skateboard carefully by her side.

She met the head squirrel's fierce gaze.

"Scruff," she said. "We've got to talk."

12

Showdown at
West 72nd Street

"TALK!" Scruff exclaimed, turning to Franklin. "If she thinks I'm going to talk to her, she's got another think coming!"

But the pigeon stood silent, surveying the hordes of people pushing and shoving their way along Central Park West to see what would happen.

"Scruff," Sally went on. "I know you want the park all to yourself, but that can't be. You've got to give it up!" She looked behind her. "Those people'll storm in here. They'll hurt you!"

Scruff was on all fours again. Sally could have sworn he was laughing at her.

"Can you believe the gall of the girl, Franklin?" he exclaimed, his eyes wide. "Asking me to give up our park? After all this time, you'd think she'd know me better!"

The pigeon shuddered. The enormity of the crowd terrified him.

"But Scruff," he said. "Look what we're facing. You can't really think we can hold out forever?"

Scruff bristled. "Oh, but I do. We're too strong now!"

"What about them?" the pigeon said, gesturing with his head toward the street. "That's a mob of people. And they don't exactly look friendly."

"For sure," Mort interjected. "It's either give up or be trampled."

"Silence, you!"

Franklin moved closer to the squirrel.

"I know it's hard to hear, but Mort's right. It's time we stop fooling ourselves. They could've stopped us the day we began. They didn't, but now they're fed up. I didn't realize how much until just now."

Ripper snorted. "Don't listen to him. He's chicken!"

"This *is* a pretty sudden turnaround, Franklin. Wasn't it this time yesterday that you led in the country birds?"

"Yes. But I didn't think about *them*," the pigeon said, looking back to the crowd. "And I got caught up by Sally's enthusiasm. I thought if we kept going, maybe we'd get something out of it."

"Oh, I see," Scruff fumed. "*Her* again! I bet that girl is at the bottom of why you want to give in now!"

Franklin took a breath. "Scruff, isn't it time you recognized a basic fact? If it weren't for *that girl*, we never would've gotten past day one. She saved your skin. She got us Corker and his troops."

"And don't forget the country birds," Mort added.

"Right," Franklin said. He looked to the edge of the park where they sat, row after row, guarding the stone wall. "Which turned out to be a pretty good idea after all."

"All right," Scruff exclaimed, waving his paws. "So the girl's helped. I admit it, okay? Satisfied? But who did what isn't of any concern anymore. What's important now, Franklin, is that you want to give up. And I still say that the girl has something to do with it."

The pigeon looked up at Sally. "Well, I won't deny one thing," he said. "If you don't at least listen to what she has to say, she'll be the laughing-stock of New York. After all, she's told everyone that she can talk to us."

Scruff's eyes blazed. "So let me get this

105

straight," he said, stepping toward the bird. "You're saying I should give up all we've done, just to spare this . . . this girl some embarrassment?"

"But it's not only for her," Franklin continued. "It's for *all* the animals. As I said, the uprising's got to end. If you stop it now, it'll end peacefully."

"But Franklin," Scruff replied, looking up the West 72nd Street line. "Do you think they've come this far to give up without a fight? I refuse to look ridiculous in front of the other animals for the sake of a girl!"

"Oh, will you be quiet," Mort cut in. "You won't look ridiculous. You'll look smart."

Scruff blinked. *"Smart?"*

"Yes, for having brains enough to scram before you get your fur whipped."

Sally was leaning forward now, trying to make out the words. She looked over her shoulder. The crowd had spilled out onto Central Park West, slowing traffic. People stood on cars, hung on lampposts, pushed against police.

"Look at that crowd, Scruff," she said. "Maybe they realize now how much they love the park. Take me. I don't know what I'd do without my skateboarding hills."

"Right," Franklin said. "Now that they've faced losing the park, maybe people will appreciate it more."

"Oh, come on!" Scruff said. "I'm certainly not going to give up this park for the sake of a notion as vague as *appreciation*! I might as well quit for nothing!" He flicked his paw. "Enough of this nonsense. I'm through with humans, and especially that girl."

The squirrel turned his back.

"Scruff!"

Sally felt tears coming.

"The squirrel refuses to talk!" a reporter yelled.

The crowd pushed farther forward, and suddenly everyone was talking at once. Then Sally heard hard footsteps on the pavement behind her. The mayor.

"He's not listening?" he asked, squatting next to her.

Sally shook her head. "No." She looked at the mayor. "I know you can't let them keep the park, but isn't there something else you can offer them?"

"Offer them?" the mayor asked. "What do you mean?"

"Well," Sally said, remembering. "The first day of the uprising, I saw Scruff grabbing at an empty grape juice container."

"Grape juice, eh? Is litter the problem?" The mayor stroked his chin. He considered running back to his deputy for advice and perhaps another doughnut, but then nodded to himself and turned again to Sally. "Scruff understands English, doesn't he?"

"Sure."

"All right, you stubborn critter," the mayor began.

Scruff peered back over his shoulder. The mayor met his glinting eyes.

"You see that line of police there?" he went on. "Well, in about two seconds I'm going to have to give them the order to drive you away. But I don't want to do that! The fact is, I'm on your side. I know as well as anyone that humans can be sloppy. Occasionally, even *I* forget to throw out my doughnut wrapping! So here's what I'm going to do: I'll put two hundred extra trash cans around the park and make every litterbug liable for a hundred-dollar fine."

Scruff didn't move.

"Not enough for you, eh?" the mayor went on. "How about this: I'll go on TV tonight and announce a citywide anti-litter campaign! Now what do ya say? Please! Look at it from my end. I can't let you keep the park. You've gotten the city's attention! There's no reason to get yourselves hurt!"

Franklin nudged Scruff. "Take his offer. He means it."

"But fast," Corker said. "If those cops come any closer, I'm scooting."

108

Before Scruff could react, Mo and Gil, the two crows from the country, swooped out of the sky and hovered above Franklin.

"Hey," Mo said. "Thanks loads for the nice time. We never knew New York was such a fun town."

"Yep," Gil said. "More fun than a barrelful of pigs at a blacksmith's."

Franklin smiled. "Glad you enjoyed our city."

"Wait a minute!" Scruff blurted. "Where do you two think you're going?"

"Home," Mo said.

"No, you're not! Get back in line!"

"Sorry," Mo drawled. "But one night's enough. Isn't that right, Gil?"

"As right as rain," Gil replied. "Why, our robin friend left an hour ago. She said she missed hearing her opera star practice so much she was suffering from—what did she call it?—oh, yeah, cultural malnourishment. And we're homesick, too. We have wives and kids, you know. And tomorrow's the cornhuskin' fair. We wouldn't miss that for the world."

With those words, the two crows flapped off for points north.

"See?" Mort said. "Your troops are deserting anyway."

"Maybe a few are. Most of those country birds'll stick it out."

Mort shook his head. "But if you think they'll fight, you're crazy!"

"No, I'm not!" Scruff ranted, raising a paw to the sky. "And if they don't want to fight, I'll . . . I'll make them! I'll never say die!"

But squads of men in blue were ready to attack the minute the mayor gave the order. Scruff couldn't deny it: his troops would be completely overwhelmed. He glanced up the blockade. How could he live with himself if any of them got hurt?

Suddenly, Sally placed her skateboard a foot away from him.

"Wanna ride?" she asked.

"Get serious!" Ripper said. "Of course he doesn't!"

But Scruff wasn't sure. A minute ago he was the very model of a fearless leader. Now he was on the verge of losing everything.

"Do it," Franklin said, fluttering down to the front of the skateboard. "We'll even get Mort."

"Oh, no, you don't," the mouse said. "As soon as this is resolved, I go straight back to my *Presidential Trivia*. I had hoped to be up to Herbert Hoover by now, but with the insanity of this week, I'm tempted to reread from Taft and his bathtub."

Scruff looked ahead at the crowd. The mayor, back with his aides now, leaned forward, biting his lower lip. Sally's father had his arm around her mother. Behind the police, hundreds and hundreds of people were waiting on his next move.

"Remember," Franklin said. "We controlled the park for four full days. That's a pretty amazing feat in itself."

The squirrel's throat was clenching, his tail twitching uncontrollably. He felt weak, yet somehow happy. Franklin was right. Whoever would have thought a group of squirrels and pigeons could take over one of the world's largest city parks?

And it hadn't all been for nothing: the mayor had made some promises. . . .

He took a final wistful look down the row of squirrels and pigeons.

"Clear a path!" he cried, wheeling around. "Clear a path!"

"It's about time," Mort said.

"Scruff!" Ripper cried. "What are you doing?"

"Letting the girl skateboard," he snapped. "What does it look like?"

Franklin was grinning. "Good for you, Scruff. Do you want to come along?"

"Are you kidding?" Scruff replied. "You still won't catch me with a human. But you go ahead. Play with the girl—I mean, Sally—for a while and then come visit me in my tree." Scruff shouted again, "Come on, everyone! You heard me! Clear a path!"

At first the animals were confused. But as soon as they realized that the decision to quit had been made, they broke ranks, feeling as relieved as Scruff. They had made their stand and now could return to the less exciting, yet decidedly saner, routines of their daily lives.

Slowly, the animals parted. Suddenly giddy, Sally stepped on the back of the board.

"The animals are letting her in!" a reporter cried. "They're letting her in!"

"It's like the Red Sea!" a woman cried. "Only without the water!"

Sally's mother felt tears in her eyes. Her father and Maurice Greene shook hands. The mayor settled back on his feet and grinned ear to ear.

"Get me ten minutes of TV time tonight," he whispered to his deputy. "I've got a short speech to make."

Working extra hard to keep her balance with Franklin on front, Sally pushed off, and slowly the board snaked forward through the sea of animals.

"More room!" Scruff commanded.

The animals scattered. A flight of pigeons lifted off, followed by a nearby group of country birds. Then, a block east and a block west, two more groups spread their wings and took to the sky. The crowd cheered.

One by one and then in a mad rush, Corker, Ripper, Scamp, and the rest of the squirrels bolted. Mort bolted, too—straight back to his reading.

Sally looked over her shoulder. Scruff was standing on his hind legs, staring at her. Though it is sometimes hard to read the facial expression of a squirrel, she thought she recognized the thin trace of a smile on his lips.

Then she looked ahead. The park was beautiful, peaceful and still—a dream come true. And for a few precious minutes, until enough animals moved away for the police to allow other people in, it would be hers alone.

Grinning broadly, she pushed off again.

The skateboard picked up speed and whooshed down the hill into the park.